The Way To Write For
THE STAGE

TOM GALLACHER

Elm Tree Books • London

ELM TREE BOOKS

Penguin Books Ltd, 27 Wrights Lane, London W8 5TZ (Publishing & Editorial)
and Harmondsworth, Middlesex, England (Distribution & Warehouse)
Viking Penguin Inc., 40 West 23rd Street, New York, New York 10010, U.S.A.
Penguin Books Australia Ltd, Ringwood, Victoria, Australia
Penguin Books Canada Limited, 2801 John Street, Markham, Ontario, Canada L3R 1B4
Penguin Books (N.Z.) Ltd, 182—190 Wairau Road, Auckland 10, New Zealand

First published in Great Britain 1987 by
Elm Tree Books/Hamish Hamilton Ltd

Copyright © 1987 by Tom Gallacher

British Library Cataloguing-in-Publication Data:

Gallacher, Tom
  The way to write for the stage. —
  (The Way to write series).
  1. Playwriting
  I. Title   II. Series
  808.2   PN1661

  ISBN 0-241-12403-4
  ISBN 0-241-12404-2 Pbk

Typeset by Pioneer, Perthshire
Printed and bound in Great Britain
by Billing and Sons Ltd, Worcester

Contents

Chapter One

Of all the means by which drama is presented, the stage is the most satisfying for the author. Live actors are going to make your work real – word for word. There will be no distortion to suit the requirements of technicians and there will be no barrier of screens or microphones or receivers. Whatever you intend, it is put directly before the public.

The actors are there in person, using all their skills to make your characters equally real. It is as though you are in every one of them. And, of course, you are there as yourself when it happens.

The setting, the lighting, the costumes are all specially designed to suit your purpose. Every detail has been carefully considered. The several individual talents of a score of people have been harnessed in an effort to show your work to its best advantage.

Nor is the audience hidden away and anonymous, as they are for film, television, or radio. The audience is part of a concerted reality in the theatre. Their attention is total. You can see them smile; hear them laugh or sigh; feel directly what they feel about your play. And, at the end of each act, a share of their applause is yours.

But more rewarding than any of these things is the joy of being there as a new artistic entity comes to life, moment by moment. Your play, once it has been professionally performed, becomes a living part of the theatrical repertoire. Yet, it is not fixed on celluloid or tape. It can be done a different way, by other actors, in other theatres, in other languages. A workable play is like a child who has great potential. But this remarkable child can grow up in as many ways, and as many times, as even a promethean parent could wish.

There is a great difference, too, in the way theatre drama is regarded in comparison with other forms of writing. In films, writers are treated like dirt. In television they are considered a necessary nuisance. In the theatre – though they may not always be agreed with – they are prized; and are able to maintain complete control over what is done with their work.

Another bonus is the notice taken of results. The critical verdict is immediate. It comes next morning. The theatre is the most efficiently reviewed of all the arts. Films (and only major films at that) are lucky if the reviews appear during the month when they open. Books might be assessed within three months of publication. Television and radio plays are subject to erratic reviews or get none at all. But press space for new plays is always found. The 'notices' are out next morning. And, in cities at any rate, they are written by professional critics – not by moonlighting fellow-practitioners.

As a theatre man at heart, I've never been able to understand why novels are reviewed by other novelists. Playwrights would consider it grossly unethical to accept money for criticising the work of their peers.

A rewarding consequence of immediate critical response is the interest it arouses from other theatres. This again is something peculiar to the stage. You may be sure that even if your television play gets an ecstatic review, no other television company will touch it. The same is true on radio. In the theatre, though, reaction is quite positively different. If your play gets rave notices there will be several phone calls before lunch time from other theatres who want to discuss their own productions of the same piece.

There are scores of professional theatres in Britain and hundreds more in Europe. The market for good workable plays is wide. For the first company to produce a new play does not own it. They have paid you only for the licence to mount one production. In repertory theatres, when that production has finished its run, the property is yours again. In commercial theatres the contract may include a subsequent tour. But, generally speaking, if the play is not in production you are free to offer it for production wherever you choose.

If one compares this with drama for television, the

2

disparity is glaring. A television company which buys the play buys the whole property for about seven years; and there's nothing else you can do with it. They show it maybe twice or, if you're very lucky, three times. But after the first time, you get only a proportion of the fixed original fee.

In the theatre, the fees (or royalties) are index-linked. For the author is paid a percentage of the seat price. And the seat prices in theatres go up every year. So, if your play is put on again after several years ('revived', as they say) you are likely to earn considerably more from it the second time than you did the first time; and a lot more on subsequent occasions.

Another financial advantage in writing for the stage is that the initial payment, too, is so much more favourable. Compared with, say, the advance for writing a novel the difference is remarkable. A publisher makes an advance payment on the author signing a contract, followed by another advance, usually on acceptance of the script. But these advances are set against royalties. They are *deducted* from your subsequent earnings. You don't get any more money until your novel has earned every penny of the money you have already received.

For stage plays, the largest part of the commissioning fee is *not* set against royalties. And it is non-returnable. That is, you are paid in advance so that the play gets written at all. Even a first play can enjoy this assurance, if it is commissioned through the Arts Council. Then, when it is written, you are paid more to allow the production company to stage it – once. And when it does you then get royalties. After that you can offer the play to somebody else and get paid all over again for the licence – and earn royalties, of course.

Nor is the piece limited to the stage. For though a television play cannot be done effectively on the stage, a stage play can be sold to television. It can be adapted and 'opened out', perhaps by the original author, perhaps by another writer. The same stage play can also be adapted for radio. And it can be adapted to fiction for publication as a book. I've done all these things with several stage plays of mine and found it very rewarding. Meanwhile, the original plays continue to be revived in the theatre.

3

Considering all these advantages, it may be wondered why more people don't write for the stage.

The answer is that it's very difficult to do.

Stage plays require a high degree of technical accomplishment. But the technique can be learned. This book is chiefly about the technique required to write effective, workable stage plays. To start with, it might be helpful to define some terms, areas of operation and targets. Broadly speaking, the professional theatre in Britain is divided between a small commercial sector and a large subsidised sector.

The Commercial Theatre

The commercial theatre is almost exclusively in the West End of London. It operates without public funds and strives to be profitable by keeping one play running as long as possible, as near to capacity attendance as possible, at the highest ticket prices the market will bear. Thus, the initial cost of the production is recouped by the producer – who then goes into profit; the initial capital put up by 'angels' is repaid – and they go into profit; the owner of the theatre continues to get a good rent; the actors continue to be paid; the author gets an increased royalty percentage of every ticket sold.

A further benefit to the author from a long West End run is that the play is snapped up by repertory theatres all over the country.

But if the play flops in the West End, every theatre in the country will be aware of the fact and *nobody* will want it. Moreover, the royalties to the playwright will be strictly on the basis of tickets sold.

The cast, director, stage crew and technicians of a commercial production are hired by the producer for that particular production. When the run ends, they disperse to look for other work.

The Subsidised Theatre

These, in the main are repertory theatres. They are

subsidised by the Arts Council and by their local authorities. They do not have to show a profit but they strive to avoid showing a loss. In fact, the term 'repertory' is a common misnomer. Strictly speaking, a repertory theatre is one which, during a season, presents a set number of plays in rotation using the same actors in different roles. That is, the company has those plays in its repertoire. The National Theatre, the Royal Shakespeare Company, Chichester and Pitlochry are proper repertory theatres. Nevertheless, to avoid confusion, I shall call all subsidised theatres 'repertory' theatres.

Most professional theatres are really civic theatres which employ the same group of directors, actors, crew and technicians for a whole season or for a number of seasons.

Generally speaking, the main season is from September to April but different theatres advertise their programmes in different ways. Often there is a pantomime running from December into January. A 'spring season' follows to the end of April or early May. There there is a 'summer season' to the end of August before the main season starts again.

These theatres do a series of productions, not in rotation but one after the other; each play usually runs for three or four weeks. The reason they cannot run the same play for a long time is simply that there are not enough people in the area which they serve. While one play is running, the next play is being rehearsed.

The person who decides which plays will go on is the theatre director or artistic director of the theatre. He or she may or may not direct the play themselves. If not, another director on the theatre's staff will do it.

The advantage to the playwright in the repertory set-up is that there is a guaranteed royalty. That is, a fixed sum which will be paid even if nobody comes to see the play. If, however, more people than anticipated come to see it, the extra royalty is paid as well.

It is important to decide what type and size of theatre your play is aimed at.

Proscenium Stage

All commercial theatres and most repertory theatres have

proscenium stages. A proscenium is that rectangular arch – the 'picture frame' from which the curtain, apparently, hangs and which separates the actors from the audience. It is the traditional Victorian theatre building, most often with a 'fly tower' which can lift or drop scenes out of and into view.

A convention of these theatres is that the archway through which you watch the play is really the 'fourth wall' of the set. The idea is that the actors pretend you are not there and they are really in a room enclosed on all sides. Even when the set is an exterior, such theatres work best when the actors can pretend the audience is not there. I mean, they pretend to the *audience* that they don't know. They themselves must remain keenly aware of the fact every moment they are on the stage.

For a play to work on the fairly large proscenium stage, it has to be 'big' enough in scope, treatment or substance. It must seem to fill the height and depth of space at its disposal. And it must be of a style which can be projected to the furthest reaches of the back stalls and upper gallery without seeming depleted or exaggerated.

Thrust Stage

Many modern theatres have thrust stages. There is no proscenium arch and no front curtain. The stage itself juts out into the audience which is seated on three sides. In fact, it is a great deal like the Elizabethan stage.

It works best for those plays which do not rely on realism. Didactic or historical material is suitable. The epic, picaresque, satirical and pageant all work well. Often there is a 'composite' set which will, at different times, suggest rather than define different locations to which the action moves.

Studio Stage

The studio stage came into vogue with the 'fringe theatre' movement. Often they are no more than lighted spaces on the same level as the audience which is grouped around in varying configurations.

Studio and fringe theatres are most effective when presenting plays of close interaction between very few characters. There is no room for much action and the interest must be sustained by direct emotion or psychological insight.

Choral Stage

For some reason that nobody has yet explained, public halls usually have choral stages. They seem specially designed to defeat the successful presentation of plays. They are all too wide, too high and too shallow. There is no space in the wings and access to the performing area is achieved only with the greatest difficulty.

Such stages work in favour of fashion shows and choral societies. If the playwright is lucky he will never have his work mounted on a choral stage. The lighting is laughably inadequate and the acoustics are appalling.

It is on such stages that non-professional companies are often obliged to perform. Sometimes touring professional companies must also endure them.

Types of Companies

When you have considered what type of theatre you are going to write your play for, the next thing to consider is the type of company to which you will offer it. There are permanent companies and there are seasonal companies.

The permanent companies are those which maintain a strong core of established actors over many years. Naturally, most of the actors are likely to be mature – particularly those cast in leading roles.

Seasonal companies engage their group of actors by the year or half-year to suit a more varied programme. Very often the actors employed on this short-term basis are young. Often, too, their strength is in didactic material. They delight

7

in plays which are weak on character and strong on a message – particularly if the message is *against* something.

Both permanent and seasonal companies usually have one thing in common. Their acting strength is unlikely to number more than a dozen persons and is frequently much less.

It may seem that there is a formidable conflict of choices before you even get down to starting your play. In fact, since all these possibilities exist, there is little conflict. But there is a great deal of rejection. If you don't consider the nature of the target before you loose your arrow, the target is likely to throw it right back at you with no explanation.

But the explanation is simple. Most plays which are sent back are not rejected because they are bad plays but because they were sent to the wrong place. You can make sure it's the right place if, for your first play, you aim at a theatre and a company you know.

At about the time I was invited to write this book I was already in correspondence with a new playwright about his first play. It seemed a good idea to ask him for a list of things *he* wanted to know about the craft. It's likely he asked some of the questions you want to have dealt with right away, though many of the points are covered in greater detail later in the book.

First, he commented on a few ground rules we had already established in our earlier correspondence. He wrote –

1) The layout of the typescript.
   I appreciate that presentation is immensely important. I agonised over the layout until you showed me the correct format.

2) The brevity of stage directions.
   Using published plays as exemplars can give the wrong idea. Even now, I have to go back and weed out unnecessary instructions. I think this is an area for which the formulation of a set of rules would be of enormous help.

3) What is required – and why – on the title page and the page detailing characters' names, etc.

These practical considerations I knew to be important. Fretting over the choice of a bracket, or where to position a line on the page, can waste an enormous amount of time and energy. I, certainly, do not feel I'm working at my best when, in the back of my mind, I'm worrying about the format and wondering if the way I'm setting it out makes what I intend clear enough. As soon as I knew I was doing it 'right', I was freer to concentrate on the real business – writing the actual play!

There followed this list of questions to which I have added my answers.

Q: How can you best assess how funny your comic writing is?

A: I'm afraid the only effective way lies with an audience (however small in number). You see, when you are reading the play to yourself, you are giving a perfect interpretation of the lines. An actor doing it will give *his* perfect reading, conditioned by a director who has in mind *his* perfect reading. Only the audience has no prior opinion of how the line should be delivered. And only the audience, therefore, knows how well the line succeeds. Even then, more depends on how well the actors say it than on how well you wrote it.

Q: Is it possible for a play that reads well to be disappointing on the stage? If so, why?

A: Yes. It is quite common. There is a very important reason why – and it should always be borne in mind; in various other contexts as well as this one. A play which reads very well may be *too complete*. The script leaves no room or opportunity for actors or the actors' vital contribution in performance. When everything is stated by the text actors are reduced to reciters and, quite properly, they object to that. Plays are not *meant* to be read. Their whole purpose is to be acted. Plays which are 'too complete' in this way are usually described as 'overwritten'. The fault is not that the actors may be offended. (God knows it is practically impossible *not* to offend actors.) It is that in performance there is a maddening impression of a double image. Everything, it seems, is being said or done twice. That is because the script is stating not only what the characters say, but what they do and what they think as well. On top of that, the actors are doing and thinking the same thing.

As a very basic example, consider this overwritten speech: –

GERALD   When they gave me the news that Kathy had died, I was stunned but now I am trying to behave quite normally for the sake of the children.

There are several things wrong with that. First, the grammar is too good for a man who's just lost his wife. The punctilious, 'gave me the news that Kathy had died' cannot really be acted. But 'When they . . . told me' can. The actor thinks himself back to the event and recreates the reaction which now he has difficulty even putting into words. The audience already knows that this man's wife has died. Further, we can *see* what he's trying to do. If the words tell us what he's trying to do and the actor actually does it then we have the information twice over. Let me restate the speech together with description of what the actor might do.

GERALD   When they (SHORT PAINFUL PAUSE) told me (HE SHAKES HIS HEAD) I . . . (HE CAN'T GO ON WITH THAT) (HE STRAIGHTENS UP) The children, you see (HE TAKES A SUDDEN SUSTAINING BREATH). They must depend on me now.

Of course, you would *not* give those directions in brackets. They are the actor's business. You would write the speech: –

GERALD   When they . . . told me, I . . . The children, you see. They must depend on me now.

Q: What is the ideal length of a play?

A: There are two factors here: 'running time' and 'playing time'. Running time is the overall time including intervals and breaks between scenes, etc. (All of which take longer than the stage manager claims they will.) A good average running time is two and a half hours. Playing time is reckoned roughly on 80 to 90 pages of A4 typescript in standard format. It is considered that each page will average one and a quarter minutes. In two-act plays the bladder factor operates. A lot of people in the audience have been to the bar during the interval so the second act should never run longer than one hour.

Q: Is there an easy way to work out how long your play will run on the stage?

A: While you are writing it, you can time scenes by the rough method mentioned above. When a scene is written it is best to time it by reading it and performing it (with time for actions, etc) in your mind.

Q: You have finished the first draft of your play. How do you distance yourself from it to criticise objectively what you have written? I'm in a position to have friends read-through a play. Would that be valuable do you think?

A: Some writers (like ordinary human beings, whom they closely resemble) are objective, others are subjective. You either can or cannot take a critical view of your own work.

    Most people cannot read plays with any degree of competence. They read them as they would read a book. Even so, if they like you, they are inclined to say they like the play. That is no bad thing for the writer's confidence. If your confidence is already in good nick, consult people who are *used* to reading plays; preferably someone with experience of directing them rather than acting them.

Q: What is the best way to go about getting your play performed?

A: The best way is having it commissioned in the first

place. Theatres are much more likely to put on a play they have paid for. Of course they don't always do so – even when they have paid handsomely. Apart from that method, the playwright's best bet is a director who likes the play and wants to produce it. Enthusiasm is a great mover of theatre managements. Generally, it is very important to make personal contact with somebody already employed by the theatre which you have chosen as target for your work. But first, see a lot of *their* work.

Q: Are there literary agents who deal solely with plays?

A: Indeed, there are. There is a list of them in *The Writers' & Artists' Yearbook* – which I commend to you in any case for a wealth of practical information.

Q: What is the best way to approach an agent – if that is a good idea?

A: You can just send a copy of your play to an agent. But it's unlikely that an agent will take on a writer with no record or credits or immediate prospect of production. For the new writer it must seem that trying to get an agent is very much like trying to secure a loan from a bank. You can't get it unless you can prove you don't need it. But that misjudges the function of the agent. He or she should be thought of as one thinks of a solicitor. They take care of your legal and business interests. But you have to have some business before there's anything they can do for you.

Q: I have read about leaving a dated copy of your play in the bank to prove copyright. Do you think that is worth the trouble?

A: Unlike patent, there is no need to prove copyright. It is automatically established by your writing the piece. All you may need (and that is unlikely) is *evidence* of time and authorship. What you may be thinking about is prosecution for plagiarism. That is, if someone else uses your work (or substantial parts thereof), claiming it as his own. In that case it is helpful to have proof that your version of the material existed before the plagiarist's version.

12

Q: Are there any moral or social taboo subjects about which it is unadvisable to write?

A: There are no taboo subjects on the stage – except, curiously enough, advising the lieges not to vote. Since most theatres are sustained by public money granted by elected representatives of the public, those representatives are likely to take reprisals against a theatre which advocates undermining their chances of re-election. In general, though, it is not advisable to deal with subjects which large numbers of the public will not pay to watch being dealt with.

Q: Should you avoid allowing a character to speak in your own personal voice?

A: Your personal voice will come through your characters whether you aim to have them speak like you or not. If I may quote from Tom Gallacher's novel *Survivor*: – "Barbara expressed surprise. 'Are you always one of the characters in your plays?'

'I am always *all* of the characters,' said Murray. 'There's no other way it can be done.'"

Q: How do you avoid the way one character expresses himself being taken up by other characters?

A: This mimicking is a constant danger. Try imagining that the second character is *trying* to do that. Listen to them, then don't let them get away with it.

Q: Do you advocate a detailed plan of the play and its plot before you begin to write any dialogue?

A: I have found it helpful to know in general terms where the high points of a play should be, and between which characters. It also saves time (and a lot of re-writing) if you start with a structure of scenes and acts with their time of day and time lapses. If you are commissioned to write a play, this and much other information will be required in advance.

Q: How important do you think the title of a play is? Have you any advice governing its choice?

A: Curiously, the title doesn't seem to matter very much, as long as it can be thought of as somehow relevant.

13

That is, *after* the audience has seen it. Prize for ostensibly bad but insistently memorable titles goes to Tennessee Williams. He insisted on *Cat On A Hot Tin Roof, A Streetcar Named Desire* and *The Milk Train Doesn't Stop Here Anymore.* Each of these is a line within the play and there is always a dramatic charge when the title line is spoken during the performance.

Q: Is there any way you can check to avoid duplicating the name of a play, film, or book?

A: There is an excellent reference book, *The Reader's Encyclopedia,* which can be consulted. This will not preclude *all* possibilities of duplication but it will discover the ones which matter.

Q: Is there any chance of a breach of copyright by inadvertently selecting a name already in use?

A: There is no breach of copyright in using an existing title. Or, only if it might seem you are trying to delude the public that your work is an already famous work – or a stage version of it. Otherwise it's just a matter of not confusing the theatre director or the public.

Q: How do you go about choosing characters' names? Is it a random selection or do you look for names that seem to suit certain characters?

A: Characters' names should, if possible, all have a different initial letter and should not sound similar. This is vital for clear exposition. I mean, their first name, or what they are most often called by other characters. However, the full name needs extra care for this can be a matter which invites litigation. If you happen upon a real name and your character has the same occupation and criminal weakness as a public figure of that name – he or she may well sue. Apart from these technical observances, the Dickensian knack of inventing names which sound like the characters is best confined to comedy.

Q: What is the best way to establish characters' names within a play?

A: Normally by having one character address another by name when both are on the stage. But not immediately. Wait until a person has been established in the audience's attention before naming him. Similarly, it's no use telling the audience the name of someone, who hasn't yet appeared, just before he comes on. They won't remember. Do it when he's on, or has just gone off.

Q: Is there any merit in writing parts with certain actors in mind?

A: No. There might be merit in it, but no mileage. The actor you want for a particular part is *never* available – not even if you're Lerner & Loewe with the backing of a top flight Broadway producer. The actor they wanted to play Professor Higgins in *My Fair Lady* was Noel Coward.

Q: Are there any rules about the length of a single speech and, with a very long speech, are there any devices you can employ to stop the audience nodding off?

A: Audiences very rarely nod off during long speeches. Good actors won't let them. In fact the only times I've seen it happen have been during plays by Samuel Beckett. He defeats the efforts of even the best actors. That is because he doesn't give a damn about the audience – or the theatre for that matter. The secret with a long speech is to write it in such a way that the actor is able to 'discover' it, bit by bit. The thought must occur to him in one sentence which prompts him to go to the next sentence – or section. It must be 'actable', not merely 'recitable'.

Q: How important is the length of each scene?

A: I'm assuming that here you mean 'character scenes' and not 'time scenes'. The length of each scene is important to the effect of the play and the progression of the plot. For example, in television the average length of a scene between major characters is under two minutes. If you did that on the stage you'd give the impression that the action was occurring in a

15

revolving door – and it would *seem* to go on forever. On the stage, something has to happen or be advanced by a scene between major characters. And each scene has to *build*. That takes time, and skill. The average duration for such a scene on the stage is twelve minutes. The 'time scenes' are sections of the play which are separated by lapses of time. In a two-act play you may have three 'time scenes' in each act and in each 'time scene' you may have three or four 'character scenes'.

Q: How important do you consider the set of a play? Should the writer worry about visual/design problems?

A: The set of a play is very important. But the writer need not concern himself with its design as long as the setting he outlines is apt for his characters and is feasible in stage terms. It is vital, however, that the writer should determine the right *place* for his play to happen in. Let me clarify an apparent contradiction of terms. I have seen many productions of *Hedda Gabler*. Each time, the set looked different, but always it was the drawing-room of the Tesman's new home.

Q: Are the economics of a play really so important – a big cast, lavish sets, etc? Does your play have to be a masterpiece before a theatre could accept high production costs?

A: First, if your play is a masterpiece there is no theatre in Britain which will accept it until you've been dead at least twenty-five years. Apart from that, economics are central to the determination of whether or not a play will be put on. It's a matter of outlay and return. A commercial (West End or Broadway) management will spend a great deal of backers' money on a large cast, lavishly-set musical on the understanding that if it runs long enough they will make a profit. They will not spend anything near that amount on a straight play because the audience appeal is not great enough. And the return is not big enough per performance because spoken words require small theatres.

16

The subsidised theatres can afford even less. They do not have a large enough audience pool to run a play as long as the commercial theatres. The amount they can spend depends entirely on the proportion of their subsidy allocated to that production and the maximum return at the box-office for a limited run.

Q: What would you consider an acceptable maximum for cast and number of scene changes?

A: At the moment, the average cast size is seven. Often it can go to nine. It is always better to have an uneven number because with a well-integrated play the characters pair off and you are likely to require an unpaired character to bridge and link the duos.

Two sets are often taken but one is preferred. If two, the change back to the opening set should be accomplished during the performance. Otherwise it costs the earth in overtime. That is, stage crew employed after their normal working hours to set Act One again for the next performance.

Q: Is it worthwhile to keep a notebook to jot down speech patterns and figures of speech that one hears daily? Would you advocate the practice?

A: A notebook is of great value. I am still making use of notes I made thirty years ago. But it is what occurs to *you* that really matters; not what other people say. It is *the idea* that must be cherished. The 'idea' is like a marvellous theory and the play is an experiment to prove it works. Of course there can be all sorts of different experiments to prove the same theory. In literary terms, this is called 'recycling the material'. A single good idea is capable of very many versions – all of them producing separate, and increasing, fees.

In all of these answers, and through the rest of the book, it will be clear that the sort of craftmanship I am advocating is that which is relevant to mainstream, traditional theatre. The purpose in that choice is the goal of durability.

I started writing for the stage in the early 1960s. Since then I have observed many fashions which, for a time,

17

fluttered the dovecotes of the avant garde. Among the great white hopes of the 'modern' stage have been: Poetic Theatre, Surreal Theatre, The Theatre of Cruelty, The Theatre of the Absurd, Minimalist Theatre, Epic Theatre, Revolutionary Theatre, Feminist Theatre, Rock Theatre, and Nihilist Theatre. None of them has survived. And the writers who pledged their souls to such experiments haven't survived either – as writers.

The writers who have survived are those who kept in mind a wider audience than the self-regarding cliques of Hampstead or Greenwich Village. They are the writers of the mainstream, traditional theatre.

Chapter Two

It will save you a lot of time if you can determine what is a suitable stage subject and what is not. There's a lot of room for misjudgement. For example, playwright classes in the United States devote much effort to instruction on 'the dramatic subject'. But what is dramatic is not necessarily stageworthy. Radio, television and film drama all need dramatic subjects. The stage subject is more particular than any of these.

To begin with, stage plays are character based. Everything starts and ends with character. Whether they are strong or weak, funny or sad, good or bad – they must be very clearly defined and they must be both interesting and convincing. More than that, the story must arise directly from the intentions and motives of the characters and the plot must progress because they are the people they are, or wish to be.

It may seem to you that that must apply equally to other forms of drama, but frequently it does not. There have been many justly praised radio plays which were 'mood' pieces. In these what was aimed at was a well-defined impression of the whole rather than the resolution of the constituent parts. Necessarily, too, there is great emphasis on narrative style which sacrifices characterisation for clarity.

Many celebrated television plays have sought to illuminate social conditions rather than to resolve individual crises. The people in them are there for what they represent rather than for who they individually are. Often, too, they are victims of circumstances outside their control imposed by authorities we never see. There is great emphasis on movement and exterior accuracy.

The cinema, too, does that sort of thing very well. But the most successful films of the recent past have been more concerned with things than people; not to mention special effects. Almost all of the films which deal with human relationships in any depth are adaptations of successful stage plays. And of those where I've been able to make the comparison, the material always worked better on the stage.

The stage subject must be capable of full exposition, conflict and resolution through *words*. You may not summon armies to your purpose – as can be done on film. You may not show communities in turmoil, nor rapidly changing scenes, nor the juxtaposition of various situations between a number of families – as can be done on television. Everything must be done with the words of less than a dozen people in a single arena.

Words are of paramount importance, also, because there are stringent limits to what the characters can *do*. Action on the stage cannot exceed what is feasible for live actors (who are not acrobats) in a confined space. It is what the actors *say* and how they say it which becomes the action; though how they look, how they move and how they seem to feel about what is said are all very important factors.

It may seem that choosing a stage subject is exceedingly difficult but if you consider some examples it becomes plainer. The trick is to locate the *scène à faire*. It is the obligatory scene. The scene you want to write the play in order to get to. The scene which is the high point of your story. Consider these: –

1) The Hero

Suppose you have in mind a story about a real life hero. Why not Charles Lindbergh? He was the first man to fly the Atlantic non-stop, and solo. The audience will feel cheated if you do not show him flying the Atlantic. That is what Charles Lindbergh is *for*, isn't it? That is where the real conflict lies. It is Lindbergh versus the elements, tiredness, hunger and the deficiencies of his aeroplane which is the *scène à faire*. The climax is reached when he lands at Le Bourget and is welcomed by thousands of cheering people. None of this can be done convincingly on the stage. It is obviously a dramatic subject. But it is a film subject; and hugely successful with James Stewart as Lindbergh in *The Spirit of St. Louis.*

2) A Family Tragedy

You want to show the anguish of a family in consequence of some crime. Maybe you are interested in penal reform. There was a celebrated case in the United States which extended the death sentence to convicted kidnappers. The child of a wealthy young couple was kidnapped. The father of the child was an American hero. In fact, he was Charles Lindbergh.

The *scène à faire* in this case is a protracted one. It is the growing tension and dread shown by the couple after the child has been abducted. This is intercut with the police search for the kidnappers. Then there's the reaction of the neighbours as hopes are raised and dashed. The ransom of fifty thousand dollars is paid, but the little boy is murdered anyway.

All that disparate action couldn't be done very convincingly on the stage. And there is an excellent stage reason why it shouldn't be. The antagonist is missing. The kidnapper and Lindbergh do not confront each other. But it made a prizewinning television play called *The Lindbergh Baby.*

3) A Blind Ideology

A political drama may appeal to you. Not a dry documentary but something where the ideology can be characterised. Just such a subject of wide scope, marvellously crystallised in the personal philosophies of two men, immediately comes to mind. History was never so helpful in providing a *scène à faire* than in the conflict over whether or not the United States should get involved with the European war against the Nazis.

Resoundingly against Hitler was the president of the United States, Franklin D. Roosevelt. Stalwartly leading the bitter campaign to keep America out was a man who'd already shown a great deal of sympathy with the Nazis. And he was as much a national hero as Roosevelt. He was – believe it or not – Charles Lindbergh.

And this is a good stage subject because it depends upon individuals; the men themselves, their character, and what they *say*. It is absolutely central to the argument that the audience should hear what Roosevelt broadcast to the American people and the speeches Lindbergh delivered to the Nazi rallies. It is vital that we hear what they say to each other when eventually there is that confrontation in the Oval Office of the White House.

Of course there will be some exposition before we get to the main business. The audience will learn what sort of life Colonel Lindbergh led before he went to Germany to be fêted by the Nazis. We will hear of his marvellous courage in flying solo across the Atlantic and of the terrible heartbreak when his child was kidnapped and murdered.

Thus, what was essential *scène à faire* material for the film and the television play becomes only background information for the stage play. What he did, what was done to him became part of his character and, for the first time, what is most important is what he *says*.

Now, it may occur to you that if they were going to spend millions of dollars making a film about Charles Lindbergh they must have been out of their minds not to deal with the kidnap and the 'America First' campaign. But, as you will know if you've seen *The Spirit of St. Louis,* those dramatic episodes are completely ignored. The film ends soon after he makes the Atlantic crossing. That is because the film is not really about Charles Lindbergh at all. It is about private enterprise and the American do-or-die, go-getting spirit. It is an inspirational tract in which Lindbergh is a prize specimen for the purposes of a particular exercise. So, from the three scenarios outlined above, which do you think is likely to tell you most about Lindbergh, the man? I'll come back to the proposed Lindbergh stage play in Chapter Five.

Before we lose sight of the point, though, I must stress the element of confrontation. Playwrights are willing to contradict well-documented facts to get at that essential *scène à faire*. The most notorious case concerns Queen

22

Elizabeth of England and Mary Queen of Scots. There have been many plays about these royal cousins and the essential scene is the one in which they meet face to face. But in life, the plain fact is: they never met. Too often, history has no sense of drama.

Another aspect which is often present in a good stage subject is the demonstration of an idea. Usually this is more important in comedy than in drama. Often, it comes before the plot.

Take Mary Chase's gentle and delightful play *Harvey*. The basic character situation to be explored is the effect of an alcoholic on his straight-laced family and friends. Elwood P. Dowd is a sweet middle-aged man. He is courteous and charming . . . and he is an incorrigible drunk. Probably the play would have worked very well indeed without the marvellous addition of an idea made real. The idea is in the creation of Elwood's best friend and constant companion, called Harvey. For Harvey is a six-foot white rabbit, who is invisible to us.

However, he is so real to the real actor playing Elwood; and, as he moves about the set, Harvey has such tangible effects on the real actors playing the family and friends, that we are convinced he is just as real as they are. A film was made of the play and it wasn't a great success. The reason is one that must be understood if you are to make the best use of the theatre. In the film, Harvey was still as real as the other people on the screen – but the other people on the screen were not real. They never are. People on the screen are flat patterns of projected light. The sheer '*livingness*' of stage actors is one of the most potent assets available to the playwright.

And of course, in *Harvey*, the choice of personified idea is accurate. Alcoholics as far gone as delirium tremens are commonly supposed to see pink elephants. In fact they are tortured by hallucinations of vengeful demons. Mary Chase took that basic clinical dread and turned it into a wise and very amiable six-foot white rabbit.

Another example of a brilliant idea at work in stage comedy also involves invisibility. This time, an invisible wall. In Alan Ayckbourn's play, *How The Other Half Loves*, the

23

stage is divided in half to show two separate rooms. The furniture and decoration on one half of the stage is quite different from that on the other half. Two very different couples live in these rooms. There are remarkably intricate scenes which occur simultaneously; each heightening the effect of the other. Then, even the invisible wall disappears and the rooms are superimposed on each other – and so, to an hilarious extent, are the people.

Again, much of our pleasure at the comedy thus provided comes from our awareness of the live peformance. The timing and dexterity of the actors, live, with real unmanageable objects and props, introduces a sense of tension with the laughter. It is rather like watching clowns performing on a high wire, without a net.

In drama (as opposed to comedy) the idea can be equally potent. But here the heightening is more often achieved by imagery or by an extended metaphor. The progress of the plot, or the situation of the characters, is echoed at a higher level by some device or intrinsic pattern. Probably that does not explain it very well. But Ibsen's *The Wild Duck* does.

The play is about a happy family, the Ekdals. Hjalmar Ekdal is an amiable dreamer who has been set up in business by a wealthy mill-owner called Haakon Werle. Hjalmar's wife, Gina, was in service at the Werle household before she married. Now the Ekdals have a young daughter called Hedvig. Unfortunately, she is going blind. We are told the failing is hereditary.

The son of the mill-owner, Gregers, comes back to town after a long absence and falls out with his father. Then he discovers it is very likely that Hjalmar is not Hedvig's real father. Gina was probably pregnant to old Werle at the time she married Hjalmar Ekdal. And, shortly after the wedding, old Werle provided money to set up Ekdal and his new wife in business. Gregers passes this information on to his friend Hjalmar and the happy family begins to disintegrate.

The heightening of this situation is provided by the world of pretence that the Ekdals have created in their attic. There they have transformed the space into a miniature forest where they keep live animals. Chief among these is an injured wild duck. It is Hedvig's wild duck and came to them in a roundabout fashion. It was shot by Haakon Werle, but his sight was failing and he did not kill it, though he left it for dead.

When Hjalmar finds out that the child is not his, he rejects her. The girl is heartbroken and anxious to prove how much she loves the man she still thinks of as her father. Gregers has an idea how that might be done. Since Hjalmar has lost what was dearest in the world to him, he suggests that Hedvig can prove her love by destroying *her* dearest possession – the wild duck. In fact, she goes further. She shoots herself instead.

This summary leaves out a great deal but does illustrate how the exterior image is linked to the interior situation. The lie which the Ekdals are living is mirrored by the make-believe world they have created in the attic. Hedvig's failing sight is as much an injury to her as that suffered by the wild duck at the hands of Haakon Werle. And, eventually, Hedvig and the duck are interchangeable as objects in the proof of love.

But, during the play, the metaphor is brilliantly used for poignant or ironic effects, too. For example, when Gregers – the infernal truth teller – discusses the wild duck with Hedvig, we are aware that what he is saying refers directly to Hedvig herself. And what *she* says about the injured bird is a sadly accurate view of her own situation. By this means, in other plays, writers have enabled their characters to say out loud what, by their nature or through ignorance, they would not reveal at all.

Dramatic metaphor can be used to cover even greater scope. Indeed, the whole play can be a metaphor; like Arthur Miller's *The Crucible*. It was written during the early years of Senator Joseph McCarthy's notorious Senate investigations of supposed communist infiltration of the State Department. These investigations expanded into an immoral smear campaign against supposed communist sympathisers in all areas of public life. Among others, the careers of writers and artists and actors were ruined by often baseless rumour.

But Miller's play does not deal with the USA in the early 1950s. Nor did he invent a suitable situation. Instead, he made a breathtakingly effective connection. The term most often applied to the Senate investigation was 'witch-hunt', so

Miller went back to the real and terrible witch trials conducted by the church around Salem in the 1690s. The parallel could not have been more apt – or more damning of Senator McCarthy and all his vindictive crew.

A great virtue of *The Crucible* is that while combatting 1950s bigotry and hysteria it is a fine and moving play in its own right. Miller's 1690s characters have strength, courage and humour. He makes them real to us and we care about them. The proof of that is in the frequent revivals of the piece, long after Senator McCarthy and the shifty, fearful President Eisenhower have ceased to have effect on any lives.

A good English example of 'whole play' metaphor is J.B. Priestley's *An Inspector Calls*. Ostensibly, the play is about the ways in which several members of a complacent middle-class family are involved in the suicide of a simple, trusting, working-class girl. The investigation conducted by the mysterious 'inspector' is firmly based in the crime thriller convention and sustains the fascinated interest of the audience on that level. But the language and seeming omniscience of the investigator give credence to a much wider scope and purpose. Gradually he takes on the significance of an avenging angel and the play itself becomes an indictment of capitalist society.

It was Priestley, too, who made excellent use of another sort of dramatic 'idea'. In his very first play, *Dangerous Corner*, he started to explore the philosophical concept of Time, which was further pursued in *Time And The Conways* and *I Have Been Here Before*.

In each of these plays, Time is an active agent. It affects the lives of the characters and also dictates the movement of the plot or its resolution. Each play employs a different Time theory for its purpose. *I Have Been Here Before* takes up Ouspensky's 'Spiral Time' theory which suggests that we keep going over the same circle but in each succeeding life at a slightly higher level – a rising spiral, in fact. That may seem rather arcane but the title alone connects the idea to a very common human experience. Who, when visiting a house or a place for the first time, has never had the rather eerie feeling that the room or the surroundings are familiar? We often feel, however impossible it may be, that we *have* been here before – and that we know what will happen next.

The next point I want to make is roundly contested by some of my colleagues. I contend (and they deny) that a dramatic subject for the stage must always be remarkable. Further, that a stage play is *never* about ordinary people, no matter how cleverly you suggest that it is.

I think that the rest of this book will give you some evidence to suggest I'm right. As you continue reading, ask yourself what possible group of people in real, everyday life is so stringently bound by so many conditions as the cast of a play. More basic than that, think of the cast on the stage playing a pefectly natural, realistic, conversational scene. Compare the way they talk with a real group of people in a real house, with a tape-recorder running. Play the recording back in your mind. *That's* what reality sounds like. It would empty any theatre within five minutes.

The truth is that actors are much, much better at being people than people are. And the reason is – they rehearse. Then, when they come to perform (to live, that is) they are well-lit, appropriately dressed and accurately equipped for all they have to do. Moreover, they are free from doubt, fear or any unprepared intrusion. However put upon, they are invulnerable to anything which is not in the script.

They are also dramatic. Why else would you have them in a play? But how many of the ordinary people you know have dramatic lives? There is just no point in writing a stage play about people to whom nothing particularly interesting happens. That's what television does so well; and, unfortunately, most novels.

All this is to suggest that in choosing a dramatic subject you take the elementary precaution of making sure it *is* dramatic; or funny; or moving; or illuminating; or even inspirational. Any of these, or some combination of them, should be available to the audience. For it is a special audience. They've taken a lot of trouble to get there. Going to the theatre is still 'an occasion'. What is presented to them in these circumstances has to be remarkable even to make it worthwhile.

Chapter Three

When you have decided what your play is going to be about and satisfied yourself that you've chosen a suitable stage subject, things start to get easier. And you will be able to see the project more clearly if you examine what you have in mind in the light of five vital questions.

The questions are: –

1)   Why does it happen to *these* people and no other?
2)   Why does it happen *here* and not elsewhere?
3)   Why does it happen *now?*
4)   What is *changed* by its happening?
5)   Why can it not happen any *other* way?

Since I've spent a lot of time and effort over the years refining and discarding suitable tests of a proposed play's viability, I am anxious that you should see how comprehensive and constructive these questions are.

Why does it happen to these people and no other?
This question is mainly to establish the size of the cast, who they are and their relationship with each other. It asks how many people you *really* need to make your play work. Most writers, when they begin to fashion plays, have an extravagant idea of how many characters they will need. For the purpose of deciding this question try not to think of them as characters. Try to think of them as interlocking components of an intricate machine.

If you have chosen a suitable stage subject you will already have reduced the possibility for error in cast size. There should not be even one character who does not in some way contribute *directly* and advance your purpose in furtherance of the plot.

And I am bearing in mind characters like the comic neighbour who may occasionally bustle in. She need have nothing to do with the plot. But she advances your purpose if she provides comic relief after a tense or sad scene between the principals. She can also pleasantly occupy stage time which will enable the next part of the main business to gather momentum. In fact, there are all sorts of functions the apparently stray character can perform. But you must know what they are before you decide to have her. *Everyone* on the cast list must earn their keep.

Of course, there are many well-known plays which do not observe that cardinal rule. But mainly they are plays which were written when actors, like other workers, were very cheap. One such play is *The Barretts of Wimpole Street* by Rudolph Besier. The writer, who was dealing with real people, knew that Elizabeth was the eldest of twelve children. Unfortunately, he put most of them in his play. They have nothing significant to do and the many brothers are all but indistinguishable one from the other. Factual accuracy does not always bestow conviction.

Getting deeper into the question, the matter of the relationship between the characters is very important. Let me give you a very basic example. Suppose you have a middle-aged woman and a teenage girl in your play. If they are strangers then you and the actresses playing them must start from scratch in establishing what sort of feeling or social attitude they have for each other. If they are teacher and pupil, some work has already been done for you. If they are mother and daughter, considerably more has been done. You see, the audience already has points of reference regarding teachers and pupils, and equally valid reference points for mothers and daughters.

I am not here advocating stereotyped relationships. *Your* teacher and pupil or mother and daughter may – and perhaps should – be very different from the usual pattern. What I'm saying is that the usual pattern gives the audience a starting point ahead of the complete strangers.

Other, more general, relationships are just as important. You can have enemy and friend, employer and employee, colleague and rival, wife and mistress, husband and lover, ruler and subject. What is useful in the mere fact of these terms is that by making a simple statement you provide instant background for the audience. You may also provide just cause for your play. For it is also true that if your characters are held together by something more than your wish to write a play about them, then it is likely to be a more cohesive play.

So far, I've been dealing with 'Why does it happen to *these* people? But you must also satisfy the rest of the question – 'and no *other?*' It may seem unfair that having provided good reason for the people who *do* appear, you must also provide good reason for those who do not.

During the performance of a play nobody walks on the stage who is not listed in the cast. At ill-managed plays I have often wondered why that was so. My uneasiness arose from the fact that the writer had not provided convincing enough reasons for the exclusion of everyone but the cast. The hazard is greatest with plays which are set in public places or the open air.

Suppose you've decided that the best place for the event is out in a street. How do you explain to the audience the absence of traffic? What excuse do you give for the fact that there are no casual passers-by? Why are there no children or stray animals? Indeed, why is it that the only people they will see are persons who have specific business in the play?

Of course, things can be better managed indoors. I'm reminded of quite a few plays which are set in a 'waiting room' of one sort or another. The symbolism of such a location is very attractive to dramatists. There are also a few which take place in bars or hotel lobbies. In order to make these venues credible the playwright is usually obliged to choose a time of day or night when such places are practically deserted.

But that fact alone imposes a condition on what type of play it will be. I mean, what sort of people must the members of the *cast* be if they hang around hotel lobbies or bars at two o'clock in the morning?

The difficulty is greatly reduced if the action of your play occurs in private accommodation or on private ground. In that case, the owner or tenant can be trusted to limit admission to the accredited cast of the play. The playwright need do no more than plant information about likely callers.

Already, I think, you can see that the choice of characters, their relationships, and why they are likely to encounter only each other, will make you consider very carefully whom you admit to the cast list.

Why does it happen here and not elsewhere?
This question has become more difficult to answer since economic circumstances have forced 'one set' plays upon the theatre. For this is the question which obliges you to define where your play is set. Some reference was made to the problem in discussing the first question. But that was to establish what people were essential or could reasonably be available. Now we must consider the place in terms of what is to happen to the people you have chosen.

It is not enough, you see, to state baldly that this is where the action occurs, take it or leave it. There must be implicit or stated reasons *why* it is happening in this particular room or place.

Suppose you have a play about two families. The husbands are business rivals, the wives are friendly with each other. Perhaps the daughter of one family is in love with the son of the other. Which house are you going to set the play in?

You don't know because I haven't given you enough information. It depends on where you can get the most to happen in a feasible way. It depends on which house is most apt for presenting the *scène à faire*. Let me give you more information.

The family with the daughter is called Brown. Mr Brown is a ruthless go-getter. He completely dominates his wife. She is a fluttery, foolish woman who thinks the world of her masterful husband. The daughter is less impressed with her father and is ready to rebel against his dislike of the young man she's in love with.

The family with the son is called White. Mr White works for the same firm as Mr Brown but he has other interests outside work. Maybe he is passionately involved with some hobby and is likely to miss out on promotion because he devotes so much energy to that. His wife is a sensible, easy-going woman. The son thinks his father has let too many chances slip. He himself is very ambitious and idealistic.

Now, do you know where you'll set the play? Will it be in

31

the Brown's house where there is likely to be more conflict? Or will it be in the White's house where there's likely to be a happy atmosphere?

Still you can't make up your mind because I have not yet told you what the play is *about*. Until you know what the play is about you are unable to decide what the *scène à faire* must be. Even with these characters and the little we know about them there are two or three directions in which the play could go. It could be a *Romeo and Juliet* conflict in which the girl and the boy are the prime movers. It could be a *Moon and Sixpence* situation in which the unlikely Mr White gets the promotion for which Mr Brown seemed the clear favourite. Then Mr White gives it all up to pursue his hobby. It could be a *School for Wives* kind of play in which the women conspire to ensure that both husbands get what they deserve – and the young lovers are happily united.

If you have been following this carefully you should have reached the following decisions. For the *Romeo and Juliet* scenario the setting should be in the Brown's house. The *Moon and Sixpence* situation would work best in the White's house because the big scene is going to be Mr White coming home to tell his family and rival he doesn't give a toss about the promotion race and Brown can have the higher position by default. The comedy conspiracy of the *School for Wives* idea would also work best in the White house because the self-possessed and confident Mrs White is more likely to offer the male-dominated Mrs Brown refuge in the first place – and set up the conspiracy.

Naturally, not all plays are set in family homes. And even with one set it is not always one household we see. There are many fine plays which have a 'composite' set – and the marvellous *Our Town* which has no set at all.

But the home of the pivotal characters does have the inbuilt advantage of seeming to need no explanation as far as the audience is concerned. Once you move away from it you have to find even better reasons for your choice. It helps a great deal if that choice seems to be dictated by the subject matter of the play.

There are, for example, a number of 'work' plays. Quite simply, the characters are there because that is where they work and what they work *at* has direct bearing on the theme of the play.

32

There are 'holiday' plays. The characters are brought together in the modest boarding house, or on the beach, or on the mountain, or aboard ship, for no better reason — initially at least — than that they have similar leisure pursuits.

There are 'crisis' plays in which refugees from some natural disaster take shelter together; 'cause' plays where some political struggle is the bond; and 'random' plays in which the characters have no idea where they are.

Apart from the random category, it should be apparent that the governing factor in choice of place is that all your characters and no others should feasibly have access to it. And it should be apt for the overall purpose of the play.

Why does it happen now?
Upon a satisfactory answer to this question depends the point at which the play opens. It is a fault of inexperienced playwrights to start the play *before* the action starts. They take an extravagant twenty minutes or half an hour to introduce characters and to explain how they got there before they even start on the subject of why the play is happening at all. By then the audience no longer cares. The action must always have started before you raise the curtain. Something interesting must already be going on which the audience tries to catch up with.

Having started at the right point, something *else* must happen within the first fifteen minutes. If it doesn't, you've lost the audience for the rest of that act. They will come back to watch the next act only if they have nothing better to do.

Within fifteen minutes must come the first turn of the screw or twist in the plot. This is called the 'hook'. It is with the hook that you catch the audience and pull at their attention until they are interested enough to go with you voluntarily. To be effective, the hook must have a marked effect on at least one of the characters already introduced.

Another short-hand term you must bear in mind is the 'trigger'. Whereas the hook is what pulls the audience before they really know what the play is about, the trigger is the actual cause of the play's unfolding. Some writers are clever enough to use hook and trigger in one device.

One of these is the most dramatic opening of any play I

know. It happens in *The Letter* by Somerset Maugham. The silence of a Malay rubber plantation is broken by a shot. As the lights go up we see the loggia of a bungalow under the trees. A man staggers into sight clutching his stomach and staggers down the stairs. A woman in her nightdress follows him out of the house. She has a revolver in her hand – and she keeps shooting at the man. Even when he's crumpled in a heap at the foot of the stairs, she keeps shooting him until the firing mechanism clicks on an empty chamber.

Another example is *The Deep Blue Sea* by Terence Rattigan. The curtain goes up on the living-room of a seedy flat and, to our astonishment, we see that there is already a character onstage. It's a woman. What is astonishing is that she is lying unconscious on the hearthrug with her head against the unlit gas fire.

In each case there is no difficulty about appreciating why the play is happening. *The Letter* opens on that night because that was the night Lesley Crosbie murdered her lover. *The Deep Blue Sea* is propelled on its course because Hester Collyer is attempting suicide. Why Lesley shot her lover and why Hester should want to commit suicide are questions which are fully explored as the plays progress. But they certainly have good reason for starting at all.

I've already mentioned *I Have Been Here Before* in connection with the theme or idea in a play. But it has a remarkably fine hook as well. The curtain goes up on a remote Yorkshire inn and it is established that there are rooms for four guests. A young man is already staying there. Then an odd foreigner, Dr Gortler, arrives looking for accommodation. He also asks about the people already in residence. He enquiries about three people: a young man and a married couple – the wife much younger than her husband. He doesn't know their names or who they are. The innkeeper's daughter is puzzled. She has no such guests and she can't put *him* up either because the three remaining rooms are already booked by three ladies.

Dr Gortler goes away murmuring that perhaps he's come on the wrong *year*. But then – five minutes into the play – comes a telephone call. It is from one of the three ladies cancelling their reservations. That is followed – nine minutes into the play – by a quite 'random' call booking two of the recently freed rooms for a man and his wife. That leaves three rooms taken and one still unexpectedly vacant – until Dr Gortler returns. The audience is hooked.

A favourite trigger of nineteenth century dramatists was the arrival of someone out of the past bearing a secret which will affect the present lives of the main characters. Even so, the person from the past must be provided with a good reason for returning at this particular moment. The device became a highly polished ritual in quite a few of Henrik Ibsen's plays. *Hedda Gabler, A Doll's House, The Wild Duck* and *John Gabriel Borkman* are all set in motion by a character who returns after long absence and insists on picking at old sores, or on redressing a balance. The high-brow expression for this interference is 'the passionate re-examination of the past'.

Prince Hamlet is shaken into action by the ghost of his father during the first scene of the play. Since the ghost is constrained to haunt Elsinore, and Hamlet has been away at university, this is the first opportunity the uneasy spirit has had since Gertrude remarried. In *Macbeth* it is the early prophecy of the witches on the heath which sets the Thane off on his bloody course to the crown. In *King Lear* it's the foolish old man's Scene 1 decision to divide his kingdom between his three daughters that sets the tragedy in train.

In modern plays the trigger is more likely to be something a character intends to do than something already done. And that leads us back to a hoary old adage attributed to Sacha Guitry – 'In the first act I tell them what I'm going to do, in the second act I tell them I'm doing it and in the third act I tell them I've done it.'

Normally it is not possible to tell the audience directly. One character has to tell another character what is afoot – and it must be told to someone who doesn't already know. Clearly, what is needed is a stranger, or a friend who's been out of touch for some time. In my own play *Revival!* that obligation is ignored. The leading actor bustles out in front of the curtain to admonish the latecomers in the audience, then tells them exactly what he has in mind for the rest of the evening. Even so, he has a good medical reason for why it is happening *now*.

Whatever device is employed it must happen as soon as possible and it must be strong enough to make the audience want to wait around to see the consequences.

What is changed by its happening?
A play is an event which happens. It is not a situation which merely exists. And, since a stage play is character based, the change must be wrought in the characters. Announcing decisive and dramatic exterior events will mean nothing to the audience unless it directly affects the individuals they've been watching. And those individuals must have had some part in bringing about, or in trying to prevent what has happened offstage.

It can affect one or more of many aspects in their lives. Their future, their happiness, their ideals, their health, their sanity, their reputation, their view of the world or their view of each other. It can affect what they (and consequently, we) see to be good or evil, just or unjust, true or false, valuable or worthless.

The same possibilities exist whether the play is farce, comedy, drama or tragedy. The loss of reputation is as effective in the bawdy comedy *Tartuffe* as it is in the powerful drama *Captain Dreyfus*. The difference is that the arch hypocrite, Tartuffe, deserved to lose his good name while the unjustly accused soldier, Alfred Dreyfus, did not. But both men end up in jail.

In both plays we see how the change is brought about; and that is important. I recall quite a few plays which were sent to me for evaluation in which the essential change was accomplished by exterior forces: –

A poverty-oppressed family was suddenly left a fortune in the will of a previously unreported uncle on the other side of the world. Even if he'd been reported early in the play it wouldn't work because the **process** which achieves the change was not put before us. The uncle, however rich and well-disposed, becomes inadmissible evidence for a theatre audience.

An eccentric inventor threatened with eviction and destitution was saved at the last moment when a huge industrial combine suddenly decided to buy one of his many patents for a huge sum. This was slightly better than the faraway uncle because the solution was **connected** to the work we see the inventor engaged upon. However, he was not engaged on the invention which was *bought*, so it wouldn't really do.

An underground resistance unit (in a Britain of the future) was bickering and losing faith in its just cause. The leader was trying his very effective best to sustain their morale against the power of the state ranged against them. A traitor was discovered and prevented from betraying the group. Things got worse. Then Britain was invaded and conquered by the Russians. There was great jubilation in the bunker and suddenly everything was sweetness and light between the members of what had been a bitter, rancorous crew. That wouldn't do – if only because the change in the persons was not accomplished by any **personal** change.

Each of the plays in these examples has a 'passive denouement'. The solution would have been achieved whether the play happened or not. A faraway rich uncle will not time his death to coincide with the last act. He will die anyway.

Much the same is true of the decisions of the big industrial company which buys the patent. Since we are not privy to their deliberations, it could be their decision to buy the patent was made before the play started. That is not our business.

When I pointed these things out to the different authors the first two accepted the point quite readily. The third author was harder to convince. In his defence he cited *Deus ex Machina*. I pointed out to him that before you may summon the god out of the machine you must put the god *in* the machine. There is a maxim for it: 'If you would knock down the Buddha, start by growing a golden fist.' The classical Greek solution will not work unless the play sets a classical Greek problem. And, in any case, the gods of the Greek theatre were not suddenly sprung upon the audience. Usually, they were there throughout the play, discussing the troubles which the foolish mortals are storing up for themselves.

In each of the above examples there is an important word printed in bold type. The words in a way define the sort of change which works on the stage. **Process, connected, personal** are really in reverse order. The change must be a personal connected process. The change affects the individual in personal terms and is brought about by something which is directly connected to the substance of the play – and the audience must be able to see the process happening.

High on anyone's list in this regard is *The Miracle Worker* by William Gibson. It is a dramatisation of the early life of the celebrated blind deaf-mute, Helen Keller. Miraculously, Miss Keller later became a writer and sought-after lecturer. The woman who taught her to speak was Annie Sullivan. In the play, Helen is a dirty, untrained, hysterically tempered seven-year-old who is a constant threat to her doting family. Annie, taking her in hand, insists upon their being isolated from the family to teach her to behave. Then child and teacher are locked in a long struggle to break through the silence and lack of sight; to connect intricate touching of hands and lip movements with separate real objects; to establish some means of communication.

At the end the child is pumping water in the yard and suddenly she connects the feeling of water with Annie's lip movements for the word, and knows that *that* is the word for the feeling, and is able to say 'water'.

Helen, therefore, is changed from a wild, ungovernable animal to a human child. And we have seen how it was accomplished, painfully, step by step. Of course the author took no credit for devising such wonderful theatrical effects. The facts came straight from Annie Sullivan's real experience and Helen Keller's diary. However, he showed remarkable skill in selecting, arranging, focusing and writing the material to make a compulsively effective play.

Why could it not have happened any other way?
Of the five vital questions this is the one which depends most on artifice. It's up to you to persuade the audience – as you go along – that the play could not unfold in any other way than the way you have chosen. This requires a great deal of ingenuity and invention. It depends on suitable answers to all of the foregoing questions. All you have at your disposal to create the inevitable is a combination of character and plot.

38

To be honest, many classics of dramatic art proceed from rather flimsy premises and even ignore their own evidence as they go along. It doesn't matter as long as the audience can be persuaded not to dwell on the inconsistencies. When *King Lear* gets going – and the callous daughters are humiliating the old king by denying him the appurtenances and style of a monarch – who remembers that the play started with Lear telling them, and us, that he was giving up his throne with the specific intention of gaining relief from the pomp and ceremony of being a king? In short, he has nothing to bitch about. But while it is happening we are on Lear's side.

Elsewhere, coincidence is in constant attendance. Many serious plays of the nineteenth century employ devices which would seem absurdly fortuitous to us, even in the lightest farce. Moreover, their leading characters are, too often, foolhardy. Figuratively speaking, the victim or heroine (instead of keeping her head down until help arrives) insists on climbing the dark stair.

That image recalls a situation which always amuses me in television drama. There, the irrational behaviour of nineteenth century characters afflicts twentieth century villains as well as heroes. When pursued on foot they always try to escape by *climbing stairs*. No real human being would do that because we are constantly aware that we cannot fly. There is just no possibility of escape from a great height.

But whereas the stark stupidity of these television characters occurs to me while I'm watching them do it, the lapses of classical drama occur to me only in retrospect. And that is the main point. Your job is to make the twists and consequences of the plot seem reasonable – if not inevitable – while it is happening.

A well-tested way of making everything seem inevitable is to start at the end and work backwards. In his excellent book, *Playwright At Work*, John van Druten quotes an amusing analysis by the critic C.E. Montague on the plays of Sardou. This takes the method to extreme lengths but does illustrate many of the essential factors which are required in plotting.

Imagine the first germ, the first thought, the very practical thought – 'What will make a good harrowing climax for Sarah Bernhardt?' Well, he might start from a standard melodramatic horror – a condemnation of the innocent to death. How, then, to sharpen its poignancy? Make the death burning; that's something. What next? Make her convict herself to save a lover. Good – what next? Make her feel that in killing herself to save her lover, she is merely leaving him in a rival's arms. Excellent! – anything more? Yes, deprive her of the consolation of knowing or hoping that the lover will ever understand her sacrifice or value her memory.

That is the way the climax of a tragic machine may be devised, by a cumulative process of invention. The climax once there, the plot issues out of it, backwards: each step 'disengages' itself. Burning? – that means the time of the Inquisition. A lover who shall be set free at a word from a mistress on trial herself and about to be burnt? Make the lady a Moor, a heathen; the man a Christian Spaniard, so framed to please the Holy Office that they will fairly jump at the chance to let him off.

But how shall she be made, while clearing him, to damn herself quite in his eyes? Nothing for it but for her to avow herself, in his hearing, as a witch, and to confess she has used hellish arts to make him fall in love with her. Yes, but she must not have verily used hellish art; else where would your audience's sympathy be?

And so, of necessity, this Moorish lady of 1517 must practice therapeutic hypnotism in order to scandalize sixteenth-century Toledo, but must also talk twentieth-century science about it so that the audience may know she is only a female Charcot, born rather soon, and not a veritable Witch of Endor. Thus are the unknown terms of Sardou's equation disengaged.

The whole of *La Sorcière* follows of its own accord.

Whereas actors nowadays are not so particular or demanding as Sarah Bernhardt, they do insist on knowing *why* the characters they are given to play behave in the way they do. It is a foolish playwright who ventures into rehearsal without cast-iron, copper-bottomed explanations for every decision or omission in the text. When they are rehearsing a part, actors display forensic skill in discovering where the inconsistencies lie.

But everything is tested in terms of the play itself. The director may quibble in general terms but the actors question only what is established by the text in hand. Thus, the eventual actions of a character can be justified – however outrageous they may be – if suitable indications are planted earlier that the character was always heading in that direction. Even a chance remark by a second character is enough to justify the first character's development; or so it seems. In fact there is no such thing as a *chance* remark in a stage play.

Nor is there a chance ailment. As someone memorably remarked about Ibsen's method, 'If a somebody sniffs in the first act, he'll catch a cold in the second, and die of pheumonia in the third.' That's exaggeration, of course, but it acknowledges Ibsen's mastery of the 'plant'. He invented the device, and a great many other devices which are almost obligatory for effective plotting.

It is the ability to 'plant' unobtrusively and well which will enable you to create inevitability. For the actors are right. Each play states its own terms and exists as a discrete structure. When you are writing the play you must ensure that the many points of progression are made clear. Then, when you have finished the play, you must go back and replant; taking out the shoots which have become redundant and putting in new ones to establish what you now know to be necessary.

If you just add new plants and leave the old ones where they are, they will cause trouble. And again it is the actors who will unerringly spot them. Not only will they spot them, they will act upon them to the dismay and confusion of all concerned. For they have the even more acute ability to know which plants were in first and to trust them above the later additions. Actors are very dangerous people to have in plays.

Chapter Four

Stage plays are divided into acts. The acts are divided into scenes. The scenes are divided into 'character scenes' or duologues. In passing, it might be worth noting that duologue applies to speeches for two people, dialogue applies to more than two.

From Shakespearean times to the early twentieth century it was quite common for plays to have four or five acts. There was also the practice, particularly in the eighteenth century, of starting a new scene whenever a new character came on, although the actual location remained the same and there was no lapse of time. In the nineteenth century the scene divisions within an act were dispensed with.

In modern plays there are usually two or three acts separated by one or two intervals: one of twenty minutes or two of about twelve minutes each. At an interval the houselights go up and members of the audience can leave their seats. The scenes during the act are separated by short pauses during which the houselights remain down and members of the audience remain in their seats.

This very basic description of the shape of a play illustrates the marked difference between an act and a scene. If the audience is going to be away for ten to twenty minutes they are going to forget what was happening and lose interest unless a distinct portion of the play has already been completed. With a scene, they merely acknowledge a time lapse in a still-developing situation.

Perhaps it will be less confusing if I concentrate first on the long-cherished three-act structure. Naturally, the particulars will vary from one play to another but the following should give a general idea of what is required.

Act One

Establish where we are. Of course, the audience can see what the place *is*. What they need to know almost immediately is *whose* place it is, or the connection between the place and the first character they see. At the same time as you are doing that, identify at least one character by name. And that need *not* be the first character they see.

Indeed, it probably won't be – for here is an odd but observable fact. It is far more likely in reality (and so on the stage) that a person entering a room will be addressed by name than that the person entering will address by name someone who is already there.

As mentioned in an earlier chapter, the business of identifying the characters and their relationship with each other is a tricky business. What must be avoided is the totally unrealistic practice of using the name of the person addressed in every second speech, question or remark. People do not do that. Listen to any conversation between two or three people and note how *rarely* it is done.

When one or two characters have been identified, leave the rest for the moment and get on into the plot. At this point you need not explain anything. Just have them talk about it. And don't start from scratch. Have the characters talk as though they are already involved. The audience will be able to latch on to the main subject, or at least to a key word. And they will actually pay more attention if things aren't spelled out too carefully at first. The *effort* to understand it obliges them to pay attention. Make them eager eavesdroppers.

Having laid some groundwork for the plot spend a little more time on specific characters who have not yet appeared. But concentrate on their relationship with the characters already met, or the threat they pose, or the expectation they arouse. There has got to be a connection with what the audience already knows.

We are now getting near the point where the 'hook' must be deployed. And that has to be set up. Again, one can't be specific because there are all sorts of hooks. But it is safe to say that something must go wrong and somebody the audience already knows must be directly affected by it. They cannot be hooked by the report of something terrible happening to somebody they haven't met.

But as soon as I wrote that I thought of *Night Must Fall*. There the 'hook' is that there are police outside the lonely cottage looking for the body of a murdered woman. Murder is a terrible enough thing to happen to anybody, but she is not in the cast. So, why should the audience care? Emlyn Williams' answer is that it affects the elderly cripple who lives in the lonely cottage – for there is a murderer loose in the area. Indeed, he comes to live in the cottage and he has the murdered woman's head in a hatbox.

Having hooked the audience you can afford to expand a bit; tell us more about the background of the characters and the situation in which they find themselves. Now, too, you can explain in more detail the mainspring of the plot. That is the 'trigger', or cause, mentioned earlier. Also, if new characters have meanwhile arrived, you can say who they are and put them to work.

Once that has been done it's time to start building to the climax at the end of the act. Generally speaking, this will be a consequence of the 'hook'. Reveal that whatever went wrong has suddenly got worse. More people are affected now and some action must be discussed or undertaken in an effort to remove the threat or improve matters. But still more complications or ramifications intrude which impose uncertainty. The strongest of these makes the Act One curtain.

The audience heads for the bar with the feeling that a fairly complete segment of the whole is within their grasp. This should be true even if the act has been split into scenes. The rough guide outlined above would be split into scenes if you needed time to elapse before a plot development could reasonably occur. For example, after the 'hook' the character directly affected could send for help to get him out of the mess, or to get some explanation of why he is in the mess. If it's going to take the helper some time to get there, or get back, you need a scene break.

But don't start the next scene with the original characters waiting for the helper to arrive. Have him already on the stage when the next scene opens. Always jump a little ahead of what the audience already knows. They won't be surprised that he's there but they would be irritated if he weren't.

44

Act Two

This is, traditionally, the 'strong' act and the event or development which ends it should be the most dramatic event in the play. Or the funniest, if it's a comedy.

Again, the act can be split into scenes to indicate lapses of time. But whereas in Act One the different scenes could be about different aspects of the plot, in Act Two all the strands have to come together. Better if all the strands have already come together, for now is no time for casual exposition. In a good Act Two the audience should be in possession of all the important material. That does not mean there will be no surprises, reverses or revelations. There should be. The better the facts or the characters have been established, the more effective such surprises will be.

So far, it may seem that I have been describing Act Two of a thriller. That is because it is in thrillers that the mechanism can be most readily seen. But it is equally true of what I think of as 'growing' plays; in which the object is to encapsulate the lives of the characters and which depend on steady development of character and situation. Such are the plays of Anton Chekhov which seem to grow in a haphazard fashion which gives a fine illusion of reality.

References to the structure of plays by Chekhov or Ibsen are complicated by the fact that they wrote four or five-act plays. To avoid confusion, I refer to the penultimate act in each case as Act Two and to the last act as Act Three – whatever its original number.

In Chekhov's most famous plays there is a pattern. Act Two is where the crisis reaches its peak. In *The Cherry Orchard,* Madame Renevskaya, the hereditary landowner, waits for news of what has become of her estate at auction. She is stunned to learn that it has been bought by the son of a serf, Lopakhin. In *Three Sisters*, it's the night of the fire when the ascendancy of their sister-in-law (one of the lower orders) is established, and news comes that the soldiers, on whom they have placed romantic hopes, are moving on. In *The Seagull,* Nina decides she will leave the young man who loves her to seek fame and romance in Moscow and the young man's mother, Madame Arkadina, decides she will return to her spendthrift lover in Paris.

Perversely, it may seem, Chekhov disguises the significance of his Act Two climaxes by constantly shifting the focus of attention to the supporting characters. There are always a lot of extra people butting in with their minor obsessions. They seem to insist that life goes on outside the main characters and that life seems to be lived in a muddle. Thus, the audience is obliged to strain its attention in order to find out what is *significantly* happening. It is an excellent device which no other writer exploited half as well.

But, however it is managed, Act Two moves inexorably towards a climax. The playwright must utilise all the resources of character, 'plants', structure, timing and place to make it as effective as possible. And yet it must clearly be understood that this is not the end of the play. When the audience goes out for the second interval they should go amazed and wondering what can possibly happen now.

Act Three

Without doubt, the most difficult act to write is Act Three of a three-act play. I'm sure that's why two-act plays achieved such rapid popularity. Playwrights everywhere saw the new form as instant salvation from a long-endured purgatory.

One consolation was that of the three acts, the last was the shortest. If the first ran fifty minutes and the second about forty minutes, then the third need be no longer than thirty minutes. Even so, that half hour probably caused more trouble than the other two put together. It's the final act that bears the brunt of the re-writes.

Things aren't so bad if the play is a thriller. Third acts are perfect for clarifying the clues and explaining the detective work. And there's scope for a final twist of the plot which unveils the unsuspected villain – who is agreeably prone to making full confessions.

In other plays, the difficulty is that the main bolt has already been shot. The *scène à faire* has already been played. All that's left is aftermath. It is damaging, also, that the second interval intrudes between the high point of the evening and the remainder. An interval is a great dissipator of tension and interest. The actors will have to fight like steers to recapture the mood of the piece. Nor are they helped, in a long play, by a distracting minority in the

46

audience worrying about how they're going to get home and frequently glancing at their watches.

That otherwise excellent playwright, James Bridie, was renowned for the weakness of his last acts. He gave the impression that, too often, he ran out of energy or interest when he came to wind up the proceedings. That is a danger, if you care more about what you can do with the characters than what's to become of them.

One solution is to bear in mind the fourth of the five vital questions set out earlier. 'What is *changed* by its happening?' It is in the final act that you have the time – and the audience has the patience – to consider all the points made in Chapter Three. And now you are at liberty to demonstrate not only what has been achieved by the action of the play but to prefigure what life is going to be like from now on as far as your characters are concerned.

It is not surprising, therefore, that the plays which have the best last acts are what I've called the 'growing' plays. Chekhov certainly reaps the benefit of his matchless technique in this regard. Perhaps I'm generalising too much but I'd say the most memorable thing about Chekhov's plays is how they end. Who can forget Madame Renevskaya saying good-bye to the house, and the past? Then hearing the first blows of the axes which will chop down her beloved cherry orchard? Or the three sisters staring into the darkening sky and sadly aware that they will never return to Moscow?

He cornered the market in failed dreams and unrealised hopes. This pervasive theme was brilliantly caught by Peter Ustinov. His pastiche in *The Loves of Four Colonels* contains what is, for me, the definitive Chekhovian line. A beautiful young woman leans against a trellis in a wilting garden. Idly she fingers her parasol. There is a long pause, then she sighs and declares to no one in particular, 'I was so looking forward to yesterday.'

Yet, for all his odd artifice, Chekhov gives a final assurance of reality. Moscow and all it implies is out of reach and even if you do get there – like Nina – things don't turn out at all well. We in the audience recognise that. It is exactly how things usually turn out for *us.*

The two-act play is structured in quite a different way; and

47

an easier way to manage. It's my opinion that if James Bridie had been able to make use of this purely technical change in the disposition of intervals his international reputation would have been greatly enhanced and he would have been a great commercial success. He wrote three-act plays because in his time that was the expected, standard practice.

The most important thing to note is that with two acts the *scène à faire* can come right at the end of the play, or anywhere from the middle of the second act to the final curtain. That makes for a strong finish. The danger is that everything until then might look like mere preparation. Such a trap must be avoided and it can be if you change your concept of what shape a play should be.

The three-act structure conforms to the traditional story format of: a beginning, a middle and an end. If that is how your play can best be realised, then that is the structure to use, regardless of fashion. But it may be you can do what you intend with a play shaped like a bridge. I mean the idea of a bridge rather than a practical one; though there are several practical bridge designs which seem ideally engineered for drama.

Imagine a rope bridge over a chasm. It starts high, droops down to the centre then slopes up again. A hump-backed bridge has the opposite profile. With Tower Bridge, the mere choice in time of crossing constitutes the danger. Whatever the shape, the idea is to devise a means of getting your characters from one side of something to the other side. What they want to get over – or overcome – can be some danger or threat in a drama; embarrassment or humiliation in a comedy; stagnation or despair in a 'growing' play.

Having only one interval around the middle of the evening also makes a good dramatic divide which invites contrasts. One thinks of two sides of an argument; the conflict of two opposing parties; Truth and Consequences; Reality and Illusion – or even Love and Marriage.

Another shape which works in two acts is the long steady climb with a rest in the middle. There the *scène à faire* would certainly occur at the end. That is very satisfying if you can bring it off, but should be attempted only by a playwright with strong nerves and a marvellous director. The reason is easily understood. The strength of the climax is like the top of a hill. But to sustain interest the plays must climb all the way up there. And if the climax isn't high enough then you have to start too low to have any hope of engaging the initial attention of the audience.

When you have decided what shape your play is to be and in how many acts, you must consider how many scenes will be necessary. There is a temptation to declare a new scene whenever there would be a lapse of time in the natural course of events.

The temptation must be resisted. A play is *not* a natural course of events. It is a very carefully arranged and deviously engineered course of events. And one of your preparatory duties is to compress time. The process is begun when you start the play with something already happening. You tell the audience that somebody is expected and, no matter how far they are supposed to have come, they actually *arrive* within twenty minutes; earlier, if they are the 'hook'.

Even during a scene there can be a great elasticity about time. Take the opening of *I Have Been Here Before* mentioned earlier. Two minutes into the playing time, Dr Gortler arrives in his car and enquires about a room. He's told there is nothing available and is directed to another boarding house further along the road, 'about five minutes by car'. He goes off to try there. The various events already mentioned take place. Then, five minutes of playing time after he went out, Dr Gortler returns. In fact, even if he'd been able to find the place without difficulty, and had as brief a conversation there as he initially had here, and had driven back again immediately – it would have taken him about fourteen or fifteen minutes. So, time is compressed into a third of its actual duration. But the audience sees nothing amiss.

In other plays, much greater feats of speed and accuracy are readily accepted. And always the need is to compress time. I cannot think of any play in which a character does something offstage which takes a *longer* playing time than would actually be required to do it.

The audience will swallow a great deal if its attention is

profitably engaged while the clock hands are spinning for offstage actions. They will be equally indulgent of events happening on the stage. This is often demonstrated in 'meal' scenes. A stage meal does not have to last nearly as long as an actual meal would. So, if you wanted to contrast the start of a happy family dinner with the disruption caused by an unwelcome visitor at the end of it, there is no need to introduce a scene break to suggest thirty minutes or more. Do the whole thing without a break in seven actual minutes.

(My own personal opinion is that you should do without the family dinner altogether. They are hell to position and direct because the only way to see all the characters is to have them strung out like The Last Supper. With that arrangement, following the dialogue makes the audience feel like spectators at a tennis match.)

Where time compression is needed, the outer world can be reported as running like a faultless, well-oiled machine. Everybody locates obscure addresses with no difficulty whatsoever, there are no delays in transit, appointments are kept on the dot, parking spaces are unfailingly vacant, people who must be called are always hovering by the phone and the public utilities send repair men *instantly*.

It is curious that although the audience will accept this unreal view of the world, they will not so readily accept perfectly valid excuses for delay – when delay suits your purpose. They themselves have to battle constantly against inefficiency and sheer bloody-mindedness in everyday life but they let their suspended disbelief drop with a clang if you use delay to cover a seam in the plot.

With the two-act structure, it is almost inevitable that you will have to split your acts into scenes. But a scene break which indicates the passage of several hours, or even days, must *itself* take time. There will be some re-arrangement of the furniture, perhaps, or the curtains which were drawn on the window for an evening scene must be opened for a day scene, or the props will have to be cleared and re-set.

While that is being done, the audience is sitting there in the dark and whatever interest or tension you and the actors have managed to build is steadily seeping away. The dark time between scenes must be kept as short as possible. The

50

stage crew will manage their part of the change with great speed. What really drags it out is the need for costume change by one or more of the actors.

You may think that a stated time lapse of a few hours won't cause problems with costumes. But it will if the few hours takes you from night to day or day to night. And you will certainly require costume changes if the scenes are a week apart.

With that in mind, it is wise to start a new scene with different characters from those who were onstage at the end of the previous scene. In that way, the actors who are to begin the new scene are ready dressed and waiting while those who ended the previous scene can use all of the gap and a few minutes into the new scene to complete their own costume change.

Considerations of this sort are part of your job. You must keep the actors-as-people in mind as well as the actors-as-characters. Also, think long and hard before you oblige the stage crew to shift large and heavy pieces of furniture during a scene break, or clear up scattered pieces of torn paper, or re-position a significant piece of bric-à-brac with great accuracy. Remember that usually the curtain will still be up and they'll be doing all these things in the dark. If you must break a vase, scatter a chess set or tear up a letter – do it just before an interval, at the end of an act.

Chapter Five

So far, and necessarily, I've been concentrating on the limitations and restrictions imposed by theatre. But there are advantages. The single greatest advantage is that the stage is manageable. Everything you ever want or need is under one roof. There is no problem of production which cannot be solved by imagination or skill. And, unlike the hazards faced by television and film directors, the weather is always exactly as you want it.

That sense of being in the right place has other advantages. A play in performance treats the audience as though they were Roman emperors. Film or television obliges the spectator to go wherever the director chooses. The watcher is rushed from place to place as though mere movement was a virtue. In the theatre, everything is brought *to* the spectator, conferring a feeling of omnipotence upon the paying customer. Whoever has business with those autocrats sitting out there in the dark must present himself for consideration on that single lighted space.

A further advantage is the sense of directness and choice. Whereas a camera will arbitrarily decide which character all of the audience must look at, in the theatre the individual members of the audience can look at whoever they please. This obliges great concentration in the actors. They have to *earn* the attention they get, from moment to moment. But since all of the actors are using your words and inhabiting characters you have created – everyone is really working for you.

With so much concentration, it is little wonder that the theatre generates stronger and more lasting images or experiences than any other drama medium. And it is capable of beauty because in the frame of the proscenium everything can be arranged to best effect with the bonus that it will be seen from a constant pre-arranged distance. The setting, the lighting and the disposition of the actors offer limitless possibilities for a live canvas.

As a playwright, you are not expected to design the set. You are expected, however, to make the right choice of where your play should happen. The place must be feasible in terms of who the characters are and it should be a place where all the characters could be required to make an appearance.

Hitherto, I've been dealing almost exclusively with plays which have one-set interiors of a single place. But there is also the widely used arrangement of a 'composite' set. That needs some explanation. For although you have undoubtedly seen one, you may not have realised the factors which govern its use.

The most effective examples are those which maintain a fairly strong unity of place. Many of Tennessee Williams' plays have composite sets. In *The Glass Menagerie* what we see is the Wingfield apartment above an alley in St Louis. There is a living-room and beyond that a dining-room. To one side, the building is cut away so that we can also see the fire-escape landing and part of the alley. At some points in the play, the apron, or front portion of the stage, becomes not only the street in St Louis but a street in other cities, too. In *A Streetcar Named Desire* the set is another corner building, this time in New Orleans. Again we see part of the street, an exterior staircase and two main rooms through the cut-away 'walls'.

Arthur Miller's *Death of a Salesman* has much the same arrangement, though here we have the back-yard as part of the composition and there is an upstairs bedroom as well as the living-room at stage level. But in this play, too, the front of the stage can be used as a non-particular place away from the leading character's home.

It will immediately occur to you that I advised against using a street and yet here are celebrated plays which break the rule. In fact, they do not. Both Williams and Miller use 'the street' as a sort of neutral zone in which their leading characters are essentially *alone*. The audience is not asked to believe that they are real streets. They are more reflections of a state of mind on which the characters unburden their thoughts. They step outside the play to do so and that idea is translated into moving out of the set.

Other composites, however, are designed to show quite separate places as real places. To accomplish this, the stage is divided into distinct 'acting areas' with some sort of background or decoration to identify the place. When the play is in progress and the action moves from, say, Berlin to Washington then the lights fade on the Berlin area and come up on the Washington area. The stage lighting takes on the role of scene-shifter as well as its many other essential duties when there is a composite set.

I mentioned Berlin and Washington because now might be a good time to give more thought to the Lindbergh stage play proposed earlier. It seems clear that it could work only with a composite set. And that may be an advantage – to reflect the divide in ideology between Roosevelt and Lindbergh with a notional divide on the stage.

But it is not enough just to divide the stage in half. For whereas Lindbergh can move freely between Berlin and Washington, Roosevelt cannot. What is more, the president is a cripple who gets about in a wheelchair. There is a further necessity imposed by exposition. Roosevelt's former life is not an ingredient of the plot, but Lindbergh's is. We have to see the hero and his wife alone together or we cannot report the past – the Atlantic flight and the kidnap of their baby. That means a hotel room in Berlin as well as the location for Nazi rallies.

Since the play is a political one we'd be unwise to ignore the people. The American people, that is. What we require is representation of the people whom these two men sought to influence on a crucial national issue. And they will try to do it by radio. Roosevelt regularly delivered his 'fireside' chats on national radio. Lindbergh broadcast too, but only on local radio in the South – which means our representative family will have to be Southerners. Thus, they'll be able to hear both men and react with each other over what they hear.

But how does all this leave our composite set? Well, we've already established what the *scène à faire* will be. That takes place in Roosevelt's office in the White House. The area showing part of a room where the Southerners group around a radio must be on the American side of the stage. On the German side we have the Lindberghs' hotel room but we do *not* have a Nazi meeting hall. Instead, we use the theatre auditorium as the hall – or even a series of halls. Lindbergh can stand in front of a Swastika set-piece at the side of the stage and address *our* audience.

That is really as much as you have to specify. What the designer will decide is what sort of arrangement will contain the various areas. Also, what sort of furniture is required and what clothes the character will wear and the props which will aid the illusion.

And if the designer has not thought of it already, the director will decide the respective sizes and stage locations of these areas.

The White House Office:	Downstage left – that is, nearest to the audience on their right. After downstage centre that's the strongest position on the stage. It is also the point where, in most theatres, actors gain access to the stage. That's important if you have an actor in a wheelchair.
Southerners' Home:	In a sort of arc upstage of office and curving towards centre. Room needn't have window because 'fireside chats' were in the evening.
Nazi Podium:	Downstage right. That means the lectern can be moved easily on and off from the wings.
Berlin Hotel Room:	Upstage of podium and curving towards centre. Useful to have window here to show view of easily identified landmark – like Brandenburg Gate or Reichstag.
Neutral Zone:	At centre line which figuratively represents the Atlantic. Therefore

nobody should walk across the centre. They must go off into wings and round back of the set. (And that takes time.)

So, it seems you can have five different places on the same stage. Indeed, you can have more than five if your stage is big enough. The important point about a composite set is that it is one unit. All of it remains in position throughout the performance. There is no time or labour involved in changing location. That is done by fading the lights up or down.

But what you gain in being able to move, at least notionally, from place to place, you lose in the number of actors any one area can hold. Characters in one part of the country cannot overlap into what is designated as another part of the country – or the world. In the Lindbergh play, the living-room of the Southerners' home would have to be larger than the Oval Office of the White House because it must accommodate three or four people whereas the office has Roosevelt alone, broadcasting; then Roosevelt and Lindbergh at the end. All they need is a desk, a couple of flags and drapes to conceal where the window would be.

Greater flexibility in composites is achieved where the play lends itself to classical treatment. For our purposes the classical treatment implies, mainly, that there will be an absolute minimum of furniture and decoration. In such a case the composite set need be no more than an artistic arrangement of steps and platforms. Here the audience identifies what the place is by the characters who appear in that particular space. Their scenes start when they walk on and end when they walk off. They talk standing up. As somebody once pertinently remarked about Shakespearean plays, 'Only the king gets to sit down.'

Few modern plays lend themselves to classical composites so, if your play requires multiple locations, you'd be wise to consider the lighting of the set. Again, you will have expert help when it comes to production but the experts should not have to spend most of their effort in overcoming your lack of forethought.

In the composite for the Lindbergh play outlined above, you will note that the components are described as forming two distinct arcs curving upstage, or away from the audience. That pattern is satisfactory because the strongest lighting in a proscenium theatre comes from the audience side of the stage. To light an upstage scene the light has to pass over a downstage scene. If the set pieces for different locations stand one behind the other a maze of shadows would be created and the actors lost.

It is possible, of course, to raise one of the locations above the other – as described for *Death of a Salesman* – but that will only work if the upper and the lower locations are in the same place; like the living-room and a bedroom in the same house. *The Miracle Worker,* too, uses that convention. Usually the lights just inside the proscenium arch are employed for the upper level.

The lights above the stage are used chiefly to illuminate the sides and back of the set and to establish apparent sources of light; like lighted lamps or sunlight streaming in through a window. Such lights cannot be used satisfactorily to illuminate actors because the actors move; and if they stand under too strong a top light their features are distorted.

These considerations are not really the playwright's business in practice. But the way in which the play is structured can certainly help in unifying the stage picture. If you have some idea of what they have to do, you will be less likely to demand the impossible. If you stipulate a location which is not really necessary to the telling of the story you are wasting lighting power and space – both precious assets with a composite set.

In general, whether the play is 'one set' or 'composite', you will have a master of stage lighting to solve your problems. Another specialist will devise and supervise sound effects. You will also have an expert in costume design. Actors do not usually wear their own clothes in a modern play and in a period play it is likely that every garment they wear will be specially designed and made for them. Very often the set and the costumes are designed by the same person but even when two people are involved they will collaborate so that the stage picture and character presentation complement each other.

Yet, on many occasions, I've seen all that expert work thrown away by the playwright. The period plays which were beautifully, accurately, set and costumed were totally undermined by sloppy text. The sloppiness was in the anachronisms. It is not enough to know, for example, when the penny post was introduced, when electric light became common for domestic interiors, or radio or telephone. There is also the obligation on the playwright to be aware of which words and phrases and speech patterns generally were *not* in use at the time when the play is supposed to be happening. If you have no ear for period speech, do not write period plays. The audience will believe in the costumes more than they believe in your characters.

The set, the costumes and the lighting do a lot more than meet the functional demands of the text. They give information and they heighten the mood and intention of the play overall.

It is not just that the characters seem to be properly dressed and inhabiting an apt place. The costumes can also tell the audience what sort of persons the characters are. We know instantly, for example, if they are rich or poor; if they are self-assured or self-effacing; if they are dominant or subservient. Changes in the costume of a particular character can instantly signal to the audience a change in his fortunes before he utters a word on the matter.

And the set design is the most potent ally the playwright can have in that nebulous area of the play's metaphor. A good designer will suggest a whole way of life for the characters and also establish at once the distinctive 'tone' which the play will adopt in dealing with its subject.

The lighting will do more than illuminate the actors. It will tell you what time of day it is. It will also suggest the mood of a particular scene – preparing the audience's mind in advance – and it will greatly enhance the metaphor, in conjunction with the setting.

All this work will be expertly done to advance your intention, even if you place obstacles in the way of the other

talents involved. The biggest obstacle is not being clear
about what you do intend. You've got to know what you
want and be able to say why you want it, though there is no
obligation to specify how it is to be managed.

If you are a new playwright, it is worth remembering that
the directors, designers and technicians are already accomplished practitioners of their particular job. They have
performed these services scores of times for writers who
were master craftsmen. So, when all's said and done, if
things don't look right or sound right with your play, it's
likely to be your own fault.

Chapter Six

Exposition starts with the preparation of the script. The first people who need information are not members of the audience but the theatre's reader, then the director, designer and production team. Your script must present all the facts they need as economically and clearly as possible.

Stage scripts are typed on one side of A4 sheets. The format, as shown in what follows, is quite different from the idiotic fashion in which publishers present plays in book form. In books, everything is jammed together: speeches, directions, tones of voice and moves. This makes the scripts practically unusable on the stage. Thus, foolishly, they reduce their sales.

The director, the assistant stage manager and the actors need plenty of blank space in which to make notes. And, since about a dozen other people apart from the cast use the script before or during production, the information *they* need must be uniformly presented.

The first page should state the name of the play, its category and the name to be given as the author, if you are using a nom de plume.

CITIZEN LINDBERGH
A Play in Three Acts

by

A.N. Other

The second title line, for another play, could be, 'A Comedy in Two Act' or 'A Farce in Three Acts'. It is assumed that if the play is in two or three acts then it is a full-length play. The only professional market for one-act plays is with fringe theatres which present lunchtime programmes. And even that market is drying up.

Elsewhere on the same page your real name and address should be given; or the name and address of your agent.

The second page is the 'set-up' page would should provide in compact form a whole range of information. Indeed, a production can be roughly costed from that page alone. As it happens, the most recent script I've been working on is an adaptation of *The Wild Duck* by Henrik Ibsen, so I shall use that as example (overleaf).

'The Wild Duck' — Set-up notes

1) This establishes the period in which the play occurs. Here, the date is important to the costume designer who must reproduce that period. If yours is a modern play, state:
TIME   Present

2) The fact that it is Norway affects both set and costume designer, and may influence casting. Your play could be in the country rather than a city, or it could be in a particular city. Give that information.

3) Here again, only the essential information is given. The note referred to is a detailed note on the set given on a different page. If your set is not complicated you can leave it entirely to the designer.
If you have two sets you must state the fact at this point. If you require a composite set state that and the main areas to be represented.

4) Stating the duration of the action gives the director a first idea of what sort of play it is. Apart from that there is the information that none of the actors will have to 'age' as they would in, say, a family saga over twenty years or more.

5) State when the first scene is to begin.

6) The time lapse of all the subsequent scenes is given in relation to the scene immediately preceding it. If you have more than one set, state which set before the reference to time lapse.

7) Here the name HJALMAR is given in capital letters because that is what he will be called throughout the text by the author. The other characters may address him as 'Ekdal' or 'Mr Ekdal'.

8) You should keep members of a family together in the cast list and state their relationship to each other as unambiguously as possible. This helps the reader remember who is who.

9) For casting reasons, the director will want to know what ages the actors are supposed to be playing. This has little to do with the real ages of the actors.

10) Add note on this page only if you think it essential. But it must be a note dealing with the mechanics or production of the play. This is no place for personal philosophising on the subject of the play or on how you came to write it. Here the note indicates that my version of the play will save the theatre a great deal of money.

'The Wild Duck'

1) **TIME**   1884

2) **PLACE**   A city in Norway

3) **SET**   The top floor studio of a portrait photographer (See note)

4) <u>ACTION</u>   The action occurs over three days

5) **ACT ONE**
          Scene 1   An evening in early spring
6)   Scene 2   Next morning

ACT TWO
          Scene 1   That afternoon
          Scene 2   Next morning

CHARACTERS

7) **HJALMAR** Ekdal   A photographer (late 30s)

8) **GINA** Ekdal   His wife (early 40s)

9) **HEDVIG** Ekdal   Their daughter (14)

Old **EKDAL**   His father (late 60s)

GREGERS Werle   A mining engineer (late 30s)

Haakon **WERLE**   His father, a millowner (mid 60s)

BERTA Sorby   Housekeeper to the elder Werle (40s)

RELLING   A doctor (40s)

MOLVIK   A former divinity student (20s)

10) <u>NOTE</u>

This adaptation dispenses with the original first act of the play and with the mansion-house set where that action occurs and with the various guests and waiters, etc. So, instead of a cast of twenty-six, of whom seventeen are extras, the cast is reduced to the nine people essential to the play. However, all the significant events of the Ibsen's Act One have been integrated into Scene 1 and Scene 2 of the present text.

T.G.

Clear exposition is essential to the audience's understanding and enjoyment of the play. You have to give them a great deal of information in a short space of time, *but* it must not be at all obvious that that is what you are doing.

Even the basic business of establishing the names of the characters needs careful consideration. It's no use relying on the programme to state the relationships between characters. Nor will the audience be guided by notes on the location or place where the action is supposed to be happening. They ignore all such information unless it comes from the stage. It often seems that the audience uses the programme only to find out how many intervals there will be.

To illustrate some of these points, there follows part of the opening scene from my play *The Only Street*. Apart from demonstrating how information is imparted to the audience, the scene will show how the typescript of a play should be laid out.

The speeches are typed single space with a double space between speeches. Vertically, there are three columns. (A) is the left-hand margin in which the characters' names are given. (B) is the tab for exits and entrances and the column where all speeches begin. The tab should be set two spaces more than the longest name on the cast list. (C) is for stage directions and should be set at centre of the text width, or a few spaces left of centre. Of course, in an actual script the columns are not lettered and the lines are not numbered.

When the curtain goes up on *The Only Street* we see a small, tatty room. There's very little furniture, and what there is looks old and broken. Most noticeable is a sagging, single bed. There is a window through which part of a row of terraced houses can be seen across the street.

So, before anything at all happens the audience already has a good idea of the milieu of the play. As soon as the characters speak it will be apparent that they are Irish. However, the accent is not heavily laid on in the text. The actors will do the accent. But the written language does have the rhythm, cadence and structural qualities of Irish speech. These provisions enable actors who are not native Irish to be convincing. The play was first presented in Dublin and there were no complaints about the veracity of the language.

'The Only Street'

TIME	Present
PLACE	Dublin
SET	The poorly furnished upstairs bedroom of a small terrace house

ACTION	The action occurs during one day
ACT ONE	A spring day from 7.00 a.m. to noon
ACT TWO	The same, from 3.00 p.m. to evening

CHARACTERS

MARTIN Doyle	A young man. Slight.
RICHARD Doyle	His elder brother. Burly.
BEATRICE Doyle	Their mother. Slovenly.
KATE Shevlin	Martin's girl. Intelligent and amused.

TITLE

The title is a quotation from a poem by Emily Dickinson called *The Only News I Know* which includes the lines:

'The only One I meet
is God — the only street,
Existence; this traversed

If other news there be
Or admirabler show —
I'll tell it you.'

1) The time of day is important for both costume and lighting.

2) 'Discovered On' is a traditional term but the information is essential. The ASM must ensure that the actor is on the set before the curtain goes up.

3) In the stage directions it helps the ASM, and the actor concerned, if the name of a character who must *do* something is given in capital letters. So, too, should offstage actions like 'There is a KNOCK at front door' or 'The CAR drives off'. The 'effects' man must be able to pick these out of the directions column.

4) State the correct sequence of events in the stage directions. In a more complicated scene it becomes crucial.

5) *Always* give the exits and entrances in the same column of the script. And underline them. These instructions are marker buoys to the ASM who has to make sure the actors are at the proper entrance and waiting to go on.

6) Again, get the sequence clear. And it helps to 'herald' an entrance or an exit in the stage directions so that a suitable cue can be established in each case. The underlined instruction marks the precise point where what may have been alluded to actually happens.

7) Having got RICHARD on at the right time we can afford to add the information for the costume designer on how he looks. It is also relevant to the plot that he is dressed for work.

8) Again, what is being *done* and information to property buyer for the bag which is essential to the plot.

9) What RICHARD is doing is separated from previous direction because he is doing it at the same time as BEATRICE goes to bag. Try to avoid mixing what, separately, characters do.

10) All the speeches in the dialogue must start in the same column and be given in lower case.

11) The two parts of BEATRICE's speech are separated by the stage direction which is in its proper column. If you mix directions in with the dialogue it makes the lines difficult to learn. The only exceptions are suggestions like (RISES) or (SITS) or (LAUGHS), e.g.
JOHN (RISING) Well, I must go.

12) The ellipsis '. . .' indicates that BEATRICE must interrupt this speech by RICHARD.

66

(A)	(B)	(C)

1

1)		<u>ACT ONE:</u> Morning.
2)		<u>MARTIN DISCOVERED ON</u>
3)		MARTIN is, apparently, asleep in the bed. He is turned on his side, facing away from us.
4)		After a moment, the bedroom door is edged open and BEATRICE peeps in.
5)		<u>ENTER BEATRICE</u>
6)		BEATRICE comes softly into the room and beckons RICHARD to follow her.
		<u>ENTER RICHARD</u>
7)		RICHARD follows her into room. He is dressed for work as a steel-erector.
8)		BEATRICE moves cautiously towards Martin's navy issue canvas hold-all. It is still packed and locked by hasp at end of zip.
9)		RICHARD approaches bed and tries to see Martin's face.
10)	RICHARD	He's dead to the world.
11)	BEATRICE	Shhhh!
		She beckons RICHARD over and they squat at the bag.
		Let him sleep.
12)	RICHARD	I've never been able to rouse him on purpose, much less . . .
	BEATRICE	Can you force that?
		She indicates clasp lock on bag. RICHARD takes out strong pen-knife to force lock.

67

'The Only Street' — Notes

1) This is a 'planted' question. First, the information that they are upstairs — because RICHARD says 'down' to the kitchen. The fact that it's an upper room is relevant to the plot. But the main 'plant' is to cover the fact that if they take the bag away we would miss the rest of their conversation.

2) BEATRICE gives a reason which is feasible enough for them to continue the conversation within our hearing. RICHARD's question was planted to elicit this answer.

3) This completes the 'plant' with some amusement. The audience's attention switches from device to character.

4) RICHARD behaves characteristically. But he also provides a prompt for the next speech.

5) The prompt is 'private'. This enables BEATRICE to respond by giving us the information that she is the mother of the figure on the bed. Her reply, also, is characteristic. But try managing this exchange without the word 'private'. It becomes more important later.

6) The reason two lines are taken here is to indicate to the actor that there is a change of thought or subject.

7) The second part of RICHARD's speech is entirely in keeping with what he is doing. But it is another prompt.

8) BEATRICE responds to it in an amusing way which tells us about RICHARD's habits but also tells us that he, too, is her son. Moreover, since she says his stuff 'used to be' spread all over the house, we can assume he does not live there any more.

9) The mystery about the figure on the bed increases. He's not just asleep — there is something <u>wrong</u>. And BEATRICE also provides a prompt. 'Letters' are important to the plot.

10) RICHARD, not much later, contradicts this statement by his actions. But the actions — when he removes and conceals a wad of letters from the bag — would not be so effective if we did not have the assertion here.

11) There follows an exchange which increases our speculation about what is wrong with the man in the bed. We are also given some hard facts about his condition.

12) It is better to leave a space than split a speech. If it is a long speech indicate that it is continued overleaf. This is very helpful to the actor when learning it, and to the ASM who is 'on the book' during performance.

2

1) RICHARD   Can we not take the bag down to the kitchen?

2) BEATRICE   What if he wakes and it's gone? He'd think
we were pryin'.

3) RICHARD   We are pryin'.

He snaps the lock.

There!

BEATRICE carefully unzips bag
and starts searching in it.

4) RICHARD   Here! Let me! They're his private things.

5) BEATRICE   What private things can he have from
his mother?

RICHARD   Things.
6)   I'll do it.

BEATRICE rises.

7)   I wouldn't let you rifle through my stuff.

BEATRICE turns away to fetch a
chair on which unpacked material
will be stacked.

8) BEATRICE   Your stuff used to be spread all over the house.
I didn't need to search for it. I tripped over it.

RICHARD removes pile of neatly
folded clothes and lays it on
chair.

RICHARD   What are we looking for?

9) BEATRICE   Some explanation, that's what. Some reason.
A letter, maybe.

10) RICHARD   I'll not go near his letters; nor will you.

11) BEATRICE   And suppose he's never able to rise again, or
speak again? How are we know the cause of it?

RICHARD   He'll be all right.

BEATRICE   He's far from all right, or I wouldn't have got
ya here before yer work. He collapsed in the
street and he's speechless.
12)   (CONTD.)

1) Though it is a continued speech, re-state the name of the character who is talking and prefix the remainder of the speech as indicated. And now we have a further piece of information. Her son was running away. But the fact that she looked in his pockets, while telling us something about her general attitude, is also another plant.

2) There follows an exchange between them which further amplifies BEATRICE's character and her relationship with RICHARD. Then she picks up the point she herself planted. She searched his pockets and found a business card. That card is germane to the plot.

3) This tells us that the brother is not properly employed, as well as RICHARD's attitude to the fact.

4) And now RICHARD removes, identifies and conceals the letters. This would not make such an impression on us without his earlier assertion. And this is the 'hook', accomplished by an action rather than a speech. We want to know more about the letters and why RICHARD is stealing them, and hiding them.

5) He says this loudly, as a sort of cover for his action.

6) RICHARD gives a prompt and also tells us something about his mother.

7) BEATRICE picks up on the prompt and expands with further reference to the mystery of the situation we are watching. Here I have used a rather florid style of speech to disguise the fact that she is really telling RICHARD what he must be aware of himself. Also, in passing she gives us the information that she has only two sons.

8) Ah! He wasn't there when the doctor called so he doesn't know what condition his brother was in earlier.

9) Clearly, it not an ordinary illness. BEATRICE reports an odd condition, 'lost and childish'. Is her son insane?

1) BEATRICE (CONTD.) Where was he goin'? That's what I want to know. There must be a ticket, or an address, in there. I've looked in his pockets.

   RICHARD Of course ya have!

2) BEATRICE Aach!

   BEATRICE cuffs the back of RICHARD's head.

   All I found was somebody else's business card.

3) RICHARD Maybe he was goin' for a real job, at last, and the thought of it overpowered him.

   BEATRICE I doubt it.

4) BEATRICE turns away and goes to look at Martin.
   Behind her back, RICHARD now draws a small bundle of airmail letters from the bag. He looks at the handwriting then quickly stuffs letter inside his shirt.

5) RICHARD And what good can it do . . .

   BEATRICE Shhh!

   She comes quickly back to close range.

6) RICHARD (SOFTLY) What good am I to do, apart from forcin' the lock — which ye've had practice in yourself?

7) BEATRICE What good? Oh, that's a rich one. That's a rich casual question to ask me. Your only brother is sick of God knows what ailment . . .

   She draws imposing breath and glances quickly over her shoulder at the bed.

   . . . and I tell you of it. And you ask me why?

8) RICHARD Well, what can I do if the doctor told ye he's just to rest?

9) BEATRICE It would take a powerful doctor to set my mind at ease — with him like that. Lost and childish again.

'The Only Street' — Notes

1) This is the start of an effective device. We fix on the name KATE.

2) BEATRICE does not answer the question but goes on talking about an earlier subject. We want to know who KATE is.

3) RICHARD pursues her line of thought when we want him to explain KATE.

4) He repeats the former question — which means it is important. But in any case we are now anxious to have the question answered.

5) BEATRICE here provides 'background' before we have the 'foreground'.

6) This is the end of the device. He tells us who KATE is. She is his brother's girl — who has been deserted, apparently.

7) Evidently BEATRICE does not approve of KATE.

8) This is a plant for the future arrival of KATE. The mere fact that RICHARD is going to tell her assures us that she will appear.

9) And, at last, we know the name of the young man in the bed. He is MARTIN. Really we should have been told his name earlier, since he's been on the stage all this time. But I could not find an apt way of naming him without drawing attention to the fact. Even here I'm not entirely happy about it so I shall introduce a joke to divert the audience's attention.

10) This impresses the name and is first line of joke.

11) BEATRICE has the punchline. It is not a big joke but it is amusing enough to move the audience once more from mechanics to character.

This opening scene between RICHARD and BEATRICE goes on for another couple of minutes, swinging back to the importance of the card she found and establishing the fact that she lives alone in this house where the brothers grew up.

When they leave the room, MARTIN wakes up and has a fairly long scene in which he re-discovers his old home, and the long stored junk of childhood.

Later, I'll set out a scene between BEATRICE and KATE when discussing the method of adapting stage work to other media. *The Only Street* became a radio play under the same title, then a television play called *The Moth and the Spiderman*, then a long story in a book called *The Jewel Maker*.

	(A)	(B)	(C)

4

RICHARD starts putting the stuff back into the bag again.

1) RICHARD   Have you told Kate?

BEATRICE does not immediately reply to that but takes over the re-folding and re-packing of the bag.

2) BEATRICE   You're sure there's no address? Or a Warrant, maybe?

3) RICHARD   Warrant! God help us, no.

He squats back on his heels.

4)   Have ye told Kate he's here?

5) BEATRICE   Isn't it Kate he's left?

6) RICHARD   She should be told. He's been living with her for . . .

7) BEATRICE   That's enough!

8) RICHARD   I'm going to tell her. I'll go by there.

BEATRICE   He's well away from her.

RICHARD   He's <u>not</u> well. That's why he's here.

9) BEATRICE   He's here because Felix brought him here in his car — thinkin' Martin was drunk.

10) RICHARD   But Martin doesn't get drunk.

11) BEATRICE   Felix refuses to believe that of anybody.

She zips bag and gets to her feet.

Well, there ye are, and we're no further forward. Not a sign. Lucky it was a friend who saw him for he carries no way of tellin' who he is. If the hospital had got hold of him, or the Garda, they'd say he was a missin' person. Or think his was the name on the card.

It will seem to you that covert exposition is very difficult to do, and I will not conceal from you that it is. In fact, there is only one easy way to do the job. But you can have *overt* exposition. To do that you need a narrator. He will tell the audience who he is, where we are, who the other people are and why we are here.

In Thornton Wilder's *Our Town* the narrator is called the Stage Manager and, apart from introducing the action, he keeps up a frequent commentary on the lives that are unfolded. He's a wise old codger, given to homespun philosophy, but he is not really personally involved as a character. In fact, his is a god-like role.

The narrator of Tennessee Williams' *The Glass Menagerie* is very different. He is the central character in the cast of four and he tells us about his family and the cost of his escape from them. The play is his personal story (largely Tennessee Williams' personal story, too) recounted from troubled memory long after the events we see.

It is always more satisfactory for the audience if the narrator is a 'real' person in the play. But that means the method of the narration must be very carefully structured. It won't do to reel off explanatory statements. The narrative passages must be considered as speeches, and not speeches in a vacuum. In fact it must seem like a duologue with the audience – though the audience does not answer back.

Here is an example, again from a play of mine. This time I'll use a modified 'publisher' format. *Revival*! is about an actor-manager turned recluse and how his wife and daughter (both actresses) cope with a curious obsession he has developed. His name is Bernard Kevin and he was a celebrated exponent of Ibsen.

The play begins when the curtains are still closed and the last of the audience is getting to their seats. Suddenly, Bernard bustles out in front of the curtain and starts chastising them. He is dressed as Ibsen's Master Builder.

(Enter Bernard)
BERNARD: *(To audience)* Aren't you ready yet? This is why the curtain goes up late you know. We're all ready on this side.

74

The . . . *(shouting)* Look at the stub. The number on the stub is the same as the number on the seat you should sit in – so sit!
(He turns away, muttering to himself)
Oh, does it matter? Does it matter?
(Direct again)
If you can find a seat, any seat – sit! You can have a brawl in the interval if you must.
(He looks all around, sighs, then smiles)
I'm sorry. All right?
(Houselights down)
I'd thought of giving you this evening as a straightforward sort of – *play*, with lots of cleverly managed but dreary exposition in the first act, two scenes in the second act set *months* apart and a tantalising question mark hanging over the final curtain.

But, tantalising or not, I do not like question marks – especially over the *final* curtain. Maybe you'd have liked it, though. That's the sort of thing my wife likes – or liked, before the Theatre went to Hell. My wife's name is Delia. Or Bernard Kevin's wife – which, probably, is what you have in the programme. For many years I was Bernard Kevin, but now I am Bygmester Solness – as you see.

'Bygmester Who?' you will say, and say you may; unless you are acquainted with High Ibsenese. Usually the title is translated as 'The Master Builder' – at some loss, I think, to the sense of it. But that needn't worry you. For the moment.

Am I too high-handed and obscure? (*He sighs*) Yes.

When the Theatre went to Hell . . . And you know when that was because you cheered it on its way – paying to see experiments. The nudity, the crudity, the cruelty and the absurdity. You supported the death of language. *I* retired into decent seclusion and thought of other things. It having become impossible to live with style, I thought of dying. With style. Dying. Not sadly, painfully, wearily, or just oldly dying; though that might be a passing necessity. But going out fully armed and competent. So few people do it well, because they do not prepare. They do not rehearse.

I left the stage and started reading philosophy so that when the time came I could fully inhabit my own spirit. In practice and in prospect, this alarmed my family. My wife it

75

alarmed because she thought my enterprise would fail. My daughter, Clare, feared that it might succeed.

(Curtain opens behind him)

And it is Clare who will shortly be seen, here, with some . . . other member of the cast to sketch in the beginning of my last act – which led to a splendid realisation.

While she is doing that . . . with this . . . other member of the cast, I'll change my clothes. That is one thing you must be careful about when dying. Be suitably dressed, because you will remain what you die *as.* If you are competent to remain at all, that is. Remember the word 'competence'. It's the hinge of the whole business.

(He is about to go off when he remembers)

Oh! The other person is my doctor. That should save them six lines at least.

(Exit Bernard)

Now, that speech does several things which narrative speeches should do. First, it reveals character. Even before the play has begun we know that Bernard is an autocratic, impatient and eccentric man. He is also an amusing man and he has established not only that the play is a comedy but that it is a theatrically stylised comedy. The speech tunes the audience in to the proper wavelength.

It also tells us about Bernard's wife, Delia: that she was his stage partner and that he is now at odds with her. And it tells us about his daughter, Clare, who seems to be more perceptive than her mother. We learn, as well, what the play is going to be about – though a mystery is implied. That is the 'hook'.

Finally, it sets up the first scene and tells us who the people are that we shall see. That scene is given in a later chapter on dialogue.

Using Bernard in this way enabled me to carry out one or two pre-emptive strikes. Since he is an actor and declares that he is the arbiter of the proceedings, he is able to make comments on the way he is doing things which forestalls the audience wondering if it could not have been better managed otherwise. The disdainful references to normal exposition, for example, disguises the fact that *he* is doing exposition.

As you can imagine, I was delighted when I hit upon this

method of opening the play. Everything is much more quickly and efficiently lined up when you have a narrator. But, out of nearly thirty stage plays, I've been able to justify a narrator on only one other occasion. That was in *Bright Scene Fading*.

And 'justify' is exactly the right word to describe what limits the use of this device. If you have one character talking directly to the audience while the rest of the cast behaves as though the audience isn't there then you must have very good reason for the anomaly.

Think of what is implicit in such an arrangement. The narrator is talking to the audience. That means he knows he is a character in a play. He knows we are in a theatre and that he's on the stage. In *The Glass Menagerie* Williams' narrator, Tom, alludes to 'the fiddle in the wings' and the *Our Town* narrator tells us he's the Stage Manager. In spite of that, these narrators are going to involve themselves in the action. Necessarily, then, what they are telling us has already happened. It stands to reason they must be remembering something or they could not tell us about it. That is exactly the stance taken by John van Druten's heroine in *I Remember Mama*. She is a writer recalling her youth which we see in flashback. The device can have great charm, but if your play requires immediacy and the tension depends on something happening *now*, do not use a narrator.

For, it also follows that when you have a narrator he or she will seem more real to the audience than the other characters. This is plainly so and relies upon the mere fact that the people in the auditorium are directly addressed – therefore the person who is talking to them must be on the same plane of reality as the individual members of that audience.

There have been plays in which the narrator was an insignificant by-stander; no more than a disinterested observer. Even so, the audience believed more in the person who was talking to them directly than in the principal characters. Curiously, the audience allied themselves with the narrator and *they* became disinterested observers. Soon they were bored observers, and the play suffered.

If you make your narrator a principal character that danger will be avoided. There are other dangers. In long solo speeches the hazard is that your narrator will seem patronising about the other characters and supercilious about the occasion. Because he or she has so much to say there could be an impression of egocentricity or conceit. Again in *Revival*! it was possible to make an asset of an inherent liability because Bernard is meant to be supercilious, egocentric and conceited. On these qualities depend his undoing and much of the comedy which follows.

Most plays just would not work with a narrator, so the difficult task of *implicit* exposition must be faced. It requires subtlety and economy. You cannot afford to slow the play down just to give background information. Whatever is happening must run on while at the same time you reveal what the audience does not know.

Even if you do not use detailed notes in writing the bulk of the play, it is wise to prepare an exposition 'check list' for the opening. The audience has three primary questions. Who are they? Where are we? What's it all about? Of course you can't answer these questions all at once or even in that order. Your check list need not be in an order of priority just as long as it contains everything of importance on one sheet for easy reference. Then you just tick the items off as you go along.

Start by listing the characters in order of appearance. You must establish their names whenever you have a suitable opportunity.

Place? – The audience will assume the first person they see belongs there unless told otherwise.

Whose place?

Why has the visitor come there?

What has happened?

Who is expected? – State position or relationship rather than by name until the audience can see them.

What is going to happen?

Names of later arrivals? – Then restate position or relationship.

Since the names of the characters are of such importance it is wise to give some thought to the names you choose. Try as far as possible to make sure that the initial, or initial sound, is different in each case. That helps exposition. There is a further advantage in these word-processor days. If your programme does 'Search & Replace' you need not type the names in column (A) for each speech: merely type a semi-colon and the lower case initial. Say the character is CHARLES, you type ;c each time, then when you've filled the memory you get the programme to turn every ;c into CHARLES.

But don't use CHARLES unless for good reasons. I've found that the dialogue is helped if you do not have names ending in 's' because the possessive case is sure to crop up. For example, 'Charles's story is certain to be spurious' will be difficult for the actor to say.

Chapter Seven

There are three basic factors which should be taken into account when writing stage dialogue: speakability, actability and continuity.

The first thing which must be stated is that accurate grammar and correct syntax are the enemies of good dialogue. I'm constantly amazed at how many writers fail to realise that the way people talk is quite different from the way in which they write. To determine this, all you have to do is listen to how people talk. Surely that's not too difficult an exercise. You need not listen to what they *say*, but you must hear the way in which they say it.

What makes good dialogue sound 'real' is largely a matter of accurately reproducing mistakes. Those mistakes are made by educated and uneducated people in conversation. Sentence structure goes to hell; there are misplaced verbs, wrongly attributed participles; subject, object and predicate are left to fend for themselves. Of course, different degrees of education or experience produce different sorts of mistakes but the overall number of them is about the same.

In stage dialogue, periods, colons, semi-colons, commas and dashes do not exist to buttress a grammatical structure. They exist as guidance marks to the actor. They indicate the length, importance and intention of short pauses. They signal changes of thought or subject direction and, above all, they reflect what the character is thinking and feeling *while* it is happening. Once you've got that firmly in mind, you are on the way to writing good dialogue.

The test for speakability can be made while it is being written. Before you write a line, speak it aloud. Listen and examine for tongue traps – those awkward combinations of letters or sounds which oblige you to take the sentence at a cautious walking pace. Remove them. Choose other words or place them in a different sequence so that the sentence can be spoken briskly and on one breath. It may not be your intention that the speech should be delivered briskly, but it should anyway be tested for speed. And actors have to breathe.

Actability is dictated by character and situation. Would this character use these words at this particular time? Does the character even know what these words *mean*? You've got to take standard of education into account as well as social position. For example there is a clearly defined mark below which nobody uses the impersonal pronoun. One has to know where that mark is. It is a long way below the royal family, though they are ridiculed for over-use of it.

At the other end of the scale, you should know that uneducated people always report in the first person; e.g. 'She said, "What are you doing here, Mrs. Drudge?" Fancy! says I, "That is just what I was goin' to ask you, Madam."' Here the exclamation, 'Fancy' is not part of what is being reported but an aside to the listener.

There are, of course, regional differences which are more subtle than accents. As a Scot, I have to be constantly on guard that I do not put a Scottish term into an English mouth. There have been many, many occasions when I've slipped up. The simple example which comes to mind is a reference to a council housing estate. That's English. We say housing scheme and for a long time, whenever it cropped up, I wrote 'scheme'.

Continuity refers not to one speech but to a sequence involving two or more characters. The necessity can be most clearly seen in a duologue and I've alluded to the mechanics of it in an earlier chapter. The invariable components are 'prompt' and 'response'.

By prompt I do not mean what happens when an actor forgets his lines. I mean something more like a tennis serve and return. Dialogue cannot proceed by a series of self-contained statements alternately spoken. What is said by one of your characters must prompt the other character to make an apt response. And the situation must be that both characters have a reason for going on with the conversation. On the stage, people have more to do with their time than listen to something which neither interests nor concerns them. Except in the plays of Bernard Shaw, of course, where most of them do nothing else.

When you want them to change the subject you arrange the line so that a character responds to his own prompt, then gives another prompt for the second character. But this internal mechanism in a single speech must also arise out of character and plot.

Something of what is involved is best shown by example. Here is the scene from *Revival*! which follows the narrator's opening speech given earlier. Clare, you remember, is the daughter of the man Dr Anstrud has come to see.

(Enter Dr Anstrud and Clare)

ANSTRUD: Yes, I did telephone once or twice. Twice. But somebody kept trying to sell me tickets.

CLARE: Tickets?

ANSTRUD: Yes, I kept getting some . . . theatre.

CLARE: This theatre.

ANSTRUD: Pardon me?

CLARE: The theatre under this flat. *(Realising)* Oh, you've only been up the private way – from the back? We're on top of a theatre. This is the old manager's apartment. Father kept it on when he sold the rest and retired.

ANSTRUD: And does he still get all his calls through the box office? The number on his card . . .

CLARE: He doesn't get any calls. He won't even *write*! That's why I have to drag up here every month to collect the allowance, when he could quite easily drop a cheque in the post and catch me where I'm at.

ANSTRUD: He does write cheques?

CLARE: Mmm?

ANSTRUD: Cheques?

CLARE: I suppose he must. To some people.

ANSTRUD: Good.

CLARE: Or maybe he doesn't believe in banks now – either.

ANSTRUD: Really.

CLARE: But he has plenty of cash. I'm surprised he still believes in doctors. Are you a real doctor?

82

ANSTRUD: How? Real?

CLARE: How indeed. He's had some weird cranks in his day. Even when I lived here. Has he had you long?

ANSTRUD: No. No, this is only my . . . Shouldn't we tell him . . . Shouldn't you, . . . I mean, I have other calls to make and if he's not at home . . .

CLARE: He *is* at home. He is *always* at home. He never leaves home.

ANSTRUD: No?

CLARE: Never in ten years since he retired from the stage. He has an attic (*she raises her arm slowly*) . . . up there.

(*Anstrud, rather awed, glances up*)

ANSTRUD: Is that right?

CLARE: Where he meditates and makes like Borkman.

ANSTRUD: Who?

CLARE: John Gabriel Borkman.

ANSTRUD: Is Mr Borkman up there?

CLARE: Who knows?

ANSTRUD: I see. Well, shouldn't you tell them . . . er, *him* . . . your father.
Why not tell him that, er . . . I'm *here*.

CLARE: Doesn't he expect you?

ANSTRUD: No, I told you. When I phoned, all I got was the offer of a single in the dress circle. But I have the laboratory reports of the tests and . . . I have to see him.

CLARE: How did you get the tests? Tests for what?

ANSTRUD: I'm sure you'll appreciate that such matters must be entirely confidential. I have to see *him*.

CLARE: You are in luck. He's expecting me; which means he will – appear. So when he comes down, or descends, shove the test tube right at him.

ANSTRUD: It's not a test tube – and I think you mean a sample bottle anyway.

CLARE: That's what I mean.

ANSTRUD: It's a preliminary report on his condition which I have to discuss in some . . . Who is this fellow Borkman?

CLARE: One of those crazy Ibsen men my father made a career of.

ANSTRUD: Ah, Ibsen. An Ibsen man.

CLARE: You know Ibsen?

ANSTRUD: I know *of* him. One of those Swedish . . .

CLARE: Norwegian.

ANSTRUD: . . . explorers.

CLARE: Playwrights.

ANSTRUD: Yes.

CLARE: Borkman was his last great success. My father's, I mean. Ibsen just went on getting crazier.

ANSTRUD: I'm glad you brought that up.

CLARE: (*on guard*) What up?

ANSTRUD: Would you say your father is . . .

CLARE: Crazy?

ANSTRUD: Not exactly.

CLARE: Not exactly crazy?

ANSTRUD: Eccentric.

CLARE: Not exactly crazy but rich.

ANSTRUD: How would you describe your father, as a person?

CLARE: Dead.

Here the prompt and response pattern is very plain. We move from 'tickets' to 'theatre' to the plot requirement of where we are. That done, back to earlier 'theatre' prompt, now disguised as 'box office' and on to character delineation. The first real change of subject comes in CLARE's speech, 'But he has plenty of cash.' Back to prompt in her own previous speech to pick up 'believe in (banks)' so that she can introduce 'believe in (doctors)'.

Aptness is illustrated first by CLARE. Her father is a famous Ibsen actor, but it is because she herself is an actress that she chooses the very apt reclusive Ibsen character 'Borkman' as example of her father's behaviour. Then ANSTRUD corrects 'test tube' to 'sample bottle' – which is the term a doctor would know and use.

Another change of subject is required to switch us from the doctor's purpose in being there back to the patient's condition. It is managed in ANSTRUD's speech by a comic jump backwards. Very businesslike, he starts off, 'It's a preliminary report on his condition which I have to discuss in some . . .' But he's out of his depth and beginning to feel vulnerable so he blurts out, 'Who is this fellow Borkman?'

Apart from the fact that the line always gets a laugh in the theatre, the dialogue is once more on the right track.

A bit further on, CLARE places prompt for changing the subject by characteristically (but unjustly) adding, 'Ibsen just went on getting crazier.' ANSTRUD leaps at it, for this is a subject he wants to get on to as a *character*. He was hoping she'd bring it up, or at least provide an opening for him to bring it up.

For some years I was employed by different theatres to deal with the writers who offered plays for production. It was my task to assess the plays and, if anything looked promising, to advise on how the script could be improved or made ready for staging. Many of the writers I wrote to or met for long discussions were offering their first play and their difficulties with such a complex craft were natural.

What struck me as quite *un*natural was an assertion which I frequently heard. Almost proudly they said, 'Of course, I never go to the theatre.' And even worse, 'Of course, I never read plays.' As politely as I could manage, I asked them how in God's name they hoped to do the job if they had no interest in how the job was done.

They protested that all my talk of prompts, responses, plants, changes of subject, characteristic speech, tones of voice and euphony were altogether more than they had bargained for when they sent me the play. They wanted the theatre to produce what they could *already* do. I had to insist that the theatre is not that hard pressed for writers.

But I tried to reassure them by pointing out that describing a procedure makes it sound much more difficult than it is. After a while, with a lot of practice in reading plays as well as writing them, the form becomes automatic. And so does the discipline over the material.

No playwright ever exerted more discipline in his work than Henrik Ibsen. Here is the first scene between NORA and CHRISTINE in *A Doll's House*. It is one of those ritual Ibsen expository scenes in which two old friends meet after a long time apart. They try to catch up with the past. This time, you try and identify the various prompts and responses and subject changes. And note, too, how character is suggested by the 'tone' of the respective participants.

(*Doorbell rings and Nora opens the door. Christine Linde, ill at ease, stands on the threshold.*)

NORA: Yes?

CHRISTINE: You don't recognise me.

NORA: No, I'm sorry, I . . . (*then incredulous*) Christine?

CHRISTINE: Yes.

NORA: Oh, how could I be so stupid? Of course! Come in. Christine! Do come in.

(*Christine advances into the room and Nora closes the door*)

That really was stupid of me. But, of course, this is such a complete surprise.

CHRISTINE: And I have changed a good deal in ten years.

NORA: No, no. It's just that . . . . Well, yes, to be honest, you have.

(*Christine laughs*)

CHRISTINE: Honest, indeed!

NORA: How long have you been in town?

CHRISTINE: I arrived this morning. On the steamer.

NORA: What a journey you must have had, in this weather. You must be exhausted. Do sit . . . But let me take your coat. Then you must sit in the warmest chair – there by the stove. How delightful it is to see you again. We certainly shall have a merry Christmas together, to make up for lost time and . . . Oh!

CHRISTINE: What is it?

NORA: Please forgive me. How could I forget. Poor Christine. Your husband . . . You are a widow now.

CHRISTINE: Yes. He died three years ago.

NORA: I didn't know it was that long, but I remember reading it in the papers. And I did mean to write to you, several times. Something always prevented me, or got in the way. I'm sorry. I should have written.

CHRISTINE: Nora, I quite understand.

NORA: How painful it must have been for you.

CHRISTINE: More hardship than pain.

NORA: Really? He didn't leave you anything?

CHRISTINE: No.

NORA: And you had no children.

CHRISTINE: No.

NORA: How sad to have nothing at all.

CHRISTINE: Not even regret. He spared me the luxury of grief, as well.

NORA: Christine!

CHRISTINE: Such things happen.

It seems that CHRISTINE is determined to say as little as possible. And that suggests this is more than just a friendly visit. Of *course* it is. Ibsen wouldn't waste our time with a mere friendly, purposeless visit. Why is CHRISTINE being so careful? NORA is put in the position of trying to squeeze information out of her former friend. We want to know what's behind it all.

But the tone of voice was what I asked you to note. NORA's tone is sympathetic and soft or bright and chatty. CHRISTINE's tone is much harder, and bitter. And that is exactly the contrast which is exploited as the scene progresses. It seems at first that CHRISTINE has had a rough time while NORA has been pampered by a doting husband. Then NORA tells her secret. The audience is astonished because they had been lulled into making a false assumption by speech pattern alone.

Ibsen never wrote a duologue in which both parties had exactly the same tone of voice or, indeed, the same point of view. There's no charge in it. Unless there is a voltage difference between two characters on the stage the current will not flow. The old master also ensured basic conflict of character (even between friendly characters) by a simple device of speech length. This excerpt is really too brief to demonstrate but overall in the NORA/CHRISTINE scenes it is NORA who does most of the talking. In the scenes between NORA and her husband, though, NORA has the short speeches.

The same disparity to a wholly different end is demonstrated in the next excerpt. It is from what is arguably the most perfect comedy in the English language, *The Importance of Being Ernest* by Oscar Wilde. Here is a proposal of marriage by Jack Worthing to Gwendolen Fairfax – an event that comes as no surprise to that most self-possessed of young ladies.

In farce, and even situation comedy, what it funny is what happens – by action and accident – to characters who sound perfectly ordinary. In verbal comedy what is funny is what the characters say. And that is the point of this excerpt. Here the dialogue is more an interrupted monologue and its purpose is not to reveal character but wholly to amuse. Yet, the artificial behaviour of the characters advances the satirical purpose of the playwright. He shows people who care more about the manner of living than living itself – and, like Gwendolen, they are quite captivating.

JACK: Miss Fairfax, ever since I met you I have admired you more than any girl . . . I have ever met since . . . I met you.

GWENDOLEN: Yes, I am quite well aware of the fact. And I often wish that, in public at any rate, you had been more demonstrative. For me you have always had an irresistible fascination. Even before I met you I was far from indifferent to you. We live, as I hope you know, Mr Worthing, in an age of ideals. The fact is constantly mentioned in the more expensive monthly magazines, and has reached the provincial pulpits, I am told; and my ideal has always been to love some one of the name of Ernest. There is something in that name which inspires confidence. The moment Algernon first mentioned to me that he had a friend called Ernest, I knew I was destined to love you.

JACK: You really love me, Gwendolen?

GWENDOLEN: Passionately.

JACK: Darling! You don't know how happy you've made me.

GWENDOLEN: My own *Ernest*!

JACK: But you don't really mean to say that you couldn't love me if my name wasn't Ernest?

GWENDOLEN: But your name *is* Ernest.

JACK: Yes. I know it is. But supposing it was something else? Do you mean to say you couldn't love me then?

GWENDOLEN: Ah! That is clearly a metaphysical speculation, and, like most metaphysical speculations, has very little reference at all to the actual facts of real life, as we know them.

JACK: Personally, darling, to speak quite candidly, I

don't much care for the name of Ernest . . . I don't think the name suits me at all.

GWENDOLEN: It suits you perfectly. It is a divine name. It has a music of its own. It produces vibrations.

JACK: Well, really, Gwendolen, I must say that I think there are lots of other, much nicer, names. I think Jack, for instance, a charming name.

GWENDOLEN: Jack? No, there is very little music in the name Jack, if any at all, indeed. It does not thrill. It produces *no* vibrations . . . I have known several Jacks and they all, without exception, were more than usually plain. Besides, Jack is a notorious domesticity for John! And I pity any woman who is married to a man called John. She would probably never be allowed to know the entrancing pleasure of a single moment's solitude. The only really *safe* name is Ernest.

JACK: Gwendolen, I must get christened at once. I mean, we must get married at once. There is no time to be lost.

GWENDOLEN: Married, Mr Worthing?

JACK: Well . . . surely! You know that I love you, and you led me to believe, Miss Fairfax, that you were not absolutely indifferent to me.

GWENDOLEN: I adore you. But you haven't proposed to me yet. Nothing has been *said* at all about marriage. The subject has not even been touched upon.

JACK: Well – may I propose to you now?

GWENDOLEN: I think it would be an admirable opportunity. And to spare you any possible disappointment, Mr. Worthing, I think it only fair to tell you quite frankly beforehand that I am fully determined to accept you.

JACK: Gwendolen!

GWENDOLEN: Yes, Mr. Worthing, what have you got to say to me?

JACK: You know what I have got to say to you.

GWENDOLEN: Yes, but you do not say it.

JACK: (*on his knee*) Gwendolen, will you marry me?

GWENDOLEN: Of course I will, darling. How long you have been about it! I am afraid you have had very little experience in how to propose.

JACK: My own one, I have never loved anyone in the

world but you!

GWENDOLEN: Yes, but men often propose for practice. I know my brother Gerald does. All my girl friends tell me so. What wonderfully blue eyes you have, Ernest! (*She sighs*) They are quite, quite blue. I hope you will always look at me just like that, especially when there are other people present.

(*Enter Lady Bracknell*)

LADY BRACKNELL: Mr Worthing! Rise, sir, from this semi-recumbent posture. It is most indecorous.

GWENDOLEN: Mamma! I must beg you to retire. This is no place for you. Besides, Mr Worthing has not quite finished yet.

LADY BRACKNELL: Finished what, may I ask?

GWENDOLEN: I am engaged to Mr Worthing, Mamma.

LADY BRACKNELL: Pardon me, you are not engaged to anyone. When you do become engaged to anyone, *I* or your father, should his health permit him, will inform you of the fact. An engagement should always come upon a young girl as a surprise, pleasant or unpleasant, as the case may be. It is hardly a matter that she should be allowed to arrange for herself. And now, I have a few questions to put to you, Mr. Worthing. And while I am making these enquiries, you, Gwendolen, will wait for me below in the carriage.

GWENDOLEN: Mamma!

LADY BRACKNELL: Gwendolen, the carriage!

GWENDOLEN: Yes, Mamma.

(*Exit Gwendolen*)

In a scene like that the characters are not governed by any need to suggest realism. They live in a world of their own and make their own rules as they go along.

A more recent playwright who devised his own reality for the sake of comedy was Joe Orton. In his plays, too, there is verbal felicity in wicked overdrive. For the rest of us, though, the stage must present a version of that world which the audience inhabits. In our dialogue, we must strive by every artifice to give the impression of ease, liveliness and conviction.

Chapter Eight

Plays unfold and progress largely by duologues between various members of the cast in different permutations. All of these duologues are heard by the audience but are secret from characters who are not party to them. That is the basic operating mode and most compelling device of stage plays. The audience is made privy to information which is secret from many of those involved. Consequently, the audience is involved. If you do not make constant use of that device then you will squander your resources.

In my experience, a lot of the trouble which new and even well-established writers have with this aspect of the job arises from the fact that they did not get satisfactory answers to the five vital questions before they began. In particular, question 2: Why does it happen *here* and not elsewhere? If you have answered that and the other questions satisfactorily you should not have too much trouble in managing the character scenes.

One of the most important things you can get your characters to do is just to come on. The first entrance of every character stimulates the audience and it is a foolish playwright who ignores the benefit of spacing the entrances for maximum effect. Thus, even when two new characters arrive together, do not bring them on together. Have one of them say the other is there and get in a bit of character building before the second one comes on.

It used to be the rule that leading actors had to have 'built' entrances. That is, the other characters would talk about them at great length before they came on – whetting the anticipation of the audience. And then, when they did appear, they got a round of applause. The 'build' is not so common now but entrance applause for star actors persists, unfortunately. They also expect a round for their final exit and require the script to make it clear that it *is* their final exit so that the audience may do the decent thing.

Even apart from star actors, the business of entrances and exits and the specific deployment of the cast must be considered very carefully. Probably the first thing to note is that there should not be a gap between the exit of one character and the entrance of another. Only on very rare occasions should the stage be empty. Nor should you leave one character treading water (or 'whistling Dixie') while he waits for the partner of his next duologue to arrive. If you have a scene between 'A' and 'B' which is to be followed by a scene between 'A' and 'C' – then 'C' should arrive before 'B' goes off. The short conversation when the three of them are on together is called a 'bridging' scene. But before 'C' arrives you should establish that 'B' *intends* to go off. I'm assuming that you have already planted the information that 'C' is due. If you like, it can come as a surprise to 'A' but not to the audience. If the play is working well, they have already suspended their disbelief.

There are universally accepted conventions which enable that suspension to succeed. All theatre audiences acknowledge that the characters do not talk to each other when they are out of sight, unless they report the conversation. Also, that when the door is closed, a stage 'room' is soundproof. Soundproof, that is, to the rest of the set but wide open to the 'fourth wall'. It is further accepted that characters will always tell the truth except when the audience *knows* they are lying. For example if 'B' is reporting to 'C' a conversation he had with 'A', he's allowed to lie as long as the audience heard the earlier conversaton and knows the truth of it. And the two versions will be stored to compare with any third version which may crop up as the play continues.

For the audience is not given all the information all at once. The playwright arranges the material in carefully controlled servings which sustain but never entirely satisfy until the end. It is rather like feeding a multi-headed monster. And once the monster's attention has been engaged it has a voracious appetite, so don't dish out thin gruel. By that I mean idle chit-chat. Get down to substantial fare right away.

92

If, for example, the incoming character has come for a showdown, start the row immediately. The cause of it or the explanation can come later.

The problem, then, is to get the right characters to talk to each other in the right order. That means plotting the character scenes. My own method for keeping tabs on the characters is to prepare a sort of horizontal bar chart on graph paper. Down the short margin I list the characters and along the top I number the pages (or minutes) of an act. Within that basic frame I plot who talks to whom and to what purpose. Only when I've got that provisionally established do I then invent the reasons why the characters arrive and depart in the required order.

And that should be the priority. Make sure of the character and plot development first, then devise the means which will enable the scheme to be carried through. If you do that you will discover you have allies on the stage. For, as the plot develops, the characters will have reasons of their own to operate the machine. If, for example, clandestine lovers want to meet they will send surplus characters away – and the reasons *they* invent need not be as good as those the playwright would otherwise have to devise because they would be inventing a lie whereas the playwright is bound to convince the audience of truth.

There are some playwrights who have absolute mastery of scene structure and some whose plays are conspicuously gerry-built. One of the masters of the business is Terence Rattigan. Let me commend to your further attention Rattigan's *The Winslow Boy*. The play is based on an actual case and is, on the face of it, an obligatory court-room drama. But Rattigan does not set it in the court-room where the exits and entrances could be determined without effort by court procedure. He sets it in the Winslow drawing-room. Thus the family and friends can be seen in a true light and the ramifications of the boy's alleged theft can be explored.

In my view, even greater mastery is displayed by the same playwright in *The Browning Version*. It is a short play – half of a double-bill – but in a hour of playing time a full-scale domestic tragedy is revealed, explored, explained and concluded. There are seven characters and the way in which they are managed – in a continuous time scale – provides an object lesson in the art.

First, he sets it in the right place – the school master's study/sitting room. And he provides himself with three doors. One is to the hallway, one to the kitchen and one is a door opening on the garden. That means those who live there can go off on the slightest pretext into the kitchen. Visitors have a choice of entry and exit. They can come in via the front door and go out by the garden, or go and wait in the garden and come in again, or go out by the front door.

The garden door is an extra refinement but, with a one-room interior, you'd be wise to provide yourself with a 'holding station' such as bathroom, kitchen, bedroom, study, attic or other offstage space where characters can be shunted until needed. Quite often when I'd almost completed a play I found that I needed another door because the pretext on which I'd got a character out of the house was not convincing enough.

You see, if a character leaves the house you need two good reasons – one for why he's leaving and an even better one for why he comes back. If he remains in the building his reasons for dropping out of sight can be as slight as the real reasons why people leave and re-enter rooms.

Of course, it is not enough to know when the characters are on, or lurking nearby. You have to know what they're doing when they are *off*. If the action of the play is confined to a short time span it is likely that their offstage activity will be linked directly to the plot. That is, they will be relieved of actually earning a living while the crisis lasts.

When the time scale is slightly longer, you have to give them occupations of some sort. Choose occupations you can make plot use of. If it can be managed, information or expertise gained at work should be pressed into service. If not, do not lumber your characters with inflexible hours, shift-work or uniforms – unless, of course, any of these can serve a specific plot purpose. In general, be specific when it's useful and vague when it's not.

If you have chosen your cast list accurately (why *these* people and no other) they will already have good reasons for both their absences and appearances. It is when the time span increases to months or even years that a strain will be placed on your powers of invention. Here the occupation is less relevant than distance. If a character has been 'in Australia for several years' the audience will consider that hindrance enough to keep him from us without speculation on what he was *doing* there. Our sole concern is getting him to make his first entrance.

In those cases the judicious 'plant', yet again, is the playwright's best friend. If you establish that a character will arrive, or even might arrive, the audience will not question the reason you've given in advance when the actual arrival occurs. But if a character arrives unheralded and you make him explain why he is suddenly there, the audience will not believe him.

This does not preclude surprise arrivals. They depend on how many of the other characters are supposed to know of the arrival. If, for example, 'B' and 'C' were not on stage when the information was planted but are the only characters on the stage when 'D' arrives – that is a complete surprise.

The fact that the audience sees all and hears all and is there all the time imposes another obligation on the playwright. You mustn't tell them the same thing twice just because two different characters need to be given the same information. When the second occasion crops up, have the tale told *off*stage, but let the audience know that is what's happening.

The question of what the individual characters know at any given point in the play is another area in which actors are marvellously skilled. It matters a great deal to them and determines how they act and react in performance. The reason they are able to spot inconsistencies is that each actor, quite properly, is thinking only of his own role. And that is a trick of concentration the playwright must learn. When you are writing the play you must be able to take the position of each character in turn. Certainly before you mark an entrance you should mentally run through what that character knows and what he thinks of what he knows. Only by that means will you be sure of his attitude and purpose on this particular entrance.

And of the two, the purpose is the more important. If you have done all the preparatory work then it is only the first entrance which needs invention. Thereafter, the characters should return because of the nature or preoccupation which you have imposed upon them. They are also constrained or obliged to behave as the plot dictates. Given that, it is just a matter of deciding in which order they should appear so that maximum tension – whether comic or dramatic – is maintained.

Chapter Nine

Before rehearsals begin, the playwright is invited to a series of pre-production discussions. First, is likely to be the question of casting. If it is a commercial project, you, the producer and the director will meet. Indeed, with a commercial management there would have been an earlier discussion between you and the producer on what director should be chosen.

The 'management' or the production company is responsible for financing the project. But once the director has been hired and the leading characters cast there is very little interference – though a representative may sit in on rehearsals. Wise managements trust their own judgement and let the director get on with it.

If it is a repertory production then the director and management representative are one. The casting is simpler, too. The director will want to use those actors already under contract to the theatre. The author may disagree in one or two instances – in which case an additional actor may be hired from outside the present company. It should be remembered, however, that the director probably agreed to put the play on bearing in mind what other plays were in the season and what actors would be cast in those plays as well as yours.

Nevertheless, the playwright is fully consulted on casting. It helps matters if you have seen the present company at work. Or you may have seen various individual actors elsewhere. What you and the director have to agree upon is what 'quality' is required in each role. The actual physical appearance is of less relevance and you must give up any idea that the picture you had in mind while writing the play is the face that must be found. It will be taken as understood that the actors proposed to you are of the right age and have the ability to represent the part.

When casting is settled, the next meeting is with the designer; or designers if costume and set are to be done by different people. The designers will have read the play with great care and have ideas on how best to advance its purpose. They will also know the particular stage they must work on. What is expected of you at this meeting is that you should give a clear idea of the 'tone' and 'ambience' of the piece – as it seems to you. State your intention clearly.

Occasionally it will be found that the three parties involved (you, the director and the designers) all have different ideas. Do not argue about it with the designers. Argue about it with the director privately. But listen carefully to the designers' view. It is their job to realise things in visual terms whereas your job is, essentially, spoken words.

A week or two later, the set designer will have a model of the proposed set and, if it is a period piece, the costume designer will have sketches to show how the characters will be dressed. Again, what is expected of you is approval of these intentions, or good reason for not approving. If the model is wildly different from what you imagined when you were writing the play, there are two possibilities. One is that you've totally failed to convey your ideas in the text; the other is that the designer knows what will work better than you do.

At this meeting, the director is the person who really has to be satisfied. He or she will have to devise and manage the movements of the entire cast before the set is built. But the questions of where the doors are going to be, the disposition of the furniture and the requirements of lighting have to be proved feasible *now*. If it seems likely that something will have to be changed, they look to you to say at once if that change is likely to affect the proper presentation of the play.

The next pre-rehearsal get-together will be much larger and before we get to that it might be helpful if I say something about the playwright's position in the theatre and about some of the other people involved.

It is generally assumed that the playwright is the equal partner of whoever is in charge. Thus, in a commercial set-up you are the equal of the producer until you start working with the director. In a repertory situation you start and remain an equal partner with the director. But the wise rule is that you actually *behave* as an equal only when you are with your partner. You do not tell anyone else to do or to stop doing anything. You must never interfere. Tell the director what you want done.

And you must separate your artistic from your business interests in the play. If you have an agent, he or she will handle everything which pertains to money. You do not raise any questions of that sort with the director, even though the director may be running the theatre as well. If you do not have an agent, you deal personally with the general manager or administrator of the theatre. Again, those discussions or arguments must never encroach upon your relationship with the director.

The stage manager (SM) is a person of great importance to your play. Once it is in performance the SM has the authority of the director and runs the whole event on the stage side of the curtain. There will usually be two assistant stage managers (ASMs) assigned to the production. One of them will be at every rehearsal working as the director's assistant and ensuring that every change, addition, movement or piece of action is logged in the script. This copy of the script will become the prompt copy and bible for the whole production and the ASM will be 'on the book'.

The other ASM is likely to be in charge of properties, called 'props', which are portable objects used by the actors in the course of the performance. Things like walking sticks, brief-cases, letters, documents, lighters or cigarettes are props.

The front of house manager (FOH) has charge of all that happens on the audience side of the curtain. The audience, publicity, ticket sales or free tickets, billing, photographs, parking spaces and bars are all under the control of the FOH manager. There may be assistants to deal with specific items related to the same area of operation.

It is likely that you will have dealings with the heads of all these departments before rehearsals begin. Probably they will attend the full production meeting. Also attending will be the director, of course, the designers, the lighting director and lighting operator.

The director will deal in turn with all these aspects of the production. Your contribution is to listen to all that is proposed and to note the various difficulties which are raised. But the protocol here, and later at rehearsals, is exact. You do not give your opinion of what are other people's jobs. Nor will anyone but the director oblige you to answer a question. Even then, the questions will relate directly to what is in the script or the possibilities of solving a problem by slight changes in the script.

Everything which is said at this meeting will reinforce a single view. They are saying, 'It is no longer *your* play, it is *our* play.' For the playwright, it is a heartening moment. After all those weeks struggling alone, suddenly he has a caring family for his child.

Finally, we get to rehearsal and you come into contact with the actors for the first time. And the contact demands great care. They will want to engage you in conversation about the part they are playing. Do not be tempted to advise them. In fact it is a golden rule that you never say anything to an actor about the play unless the director is there – and listening. Observing that rule will save a lot of heartache and tension.

It's not that actors are troublemakers, though some of them are. It is just that often they have already formed a decided opinion on how the part should be played and that opinion may be at variance with what the director intends. If you side with the actor privately, or even seem to side with them, they will use what you've said in their arguments with the director. That's no way to treat a partner.

At the first reading of a new play it's wise to bear in mind that everyone else is more nervous than you are. You are introduced to the cast, then everyone sits down in a casual group. Very often, the director will invite you to introduce the play. That is, they want to hear what you think is important or interesting about the piece. Keep your remarks short and restrict them to general observations. *Do not* give the slightest hint of opinion on how you think this or that part should be played.

If it's your first play, prepare to be shocked when they start reading it. Nothing will sound right. It will seem that every actor is taking positive delight in mucking up your lines. Occasionally, a typing error of yours will be discovered, and loudly spoken as read. Then, too, they will find speeches which have been wrongly attributed – by you. That is, you've mixed up the names of the characters. They can see that perfectly well but the wrong actor will say the line anyway. Amid all the fumbling and fluffing and two pages turned over at a time, then back-tracked, it may well occur to you that the whole enterprise is already doomed.

Eventually, it is over and they expect you to say something. Do not say, 'As God is my judge, I have never heard such a fumbling farrago of foul reading.' Say 'Thank you all very much. I am looking forward to rehearsals.'

Only when you've sat through several first readings does it become plain that the exercise has very little to do with rehearsing. It is a ritual, honoured in observance when it should be breached. But it *is* a place to begin, and we must begin somewhere.

You will be invited to attend rehearsals 'whenever you like' and the ASM will provide you with a list of the times and locations, beginning that afternoon, or next morning. Don't go. Don't go for at least a week. Give the director your telephone number so that you can be called to clarify any sticking points in the script, but stay away.

While you are blessedly out of sight, the director will be engaged first on 'blocking' the play. That is, going through it line by line to plot the moves and positions with the actors. The actors note these in their scripts and try each little section to let the director see how it looks. Sometimes it looks just fine, but most often another variation has to be tried. They will go over the same small section perhaps half a dozen times. And during all of this they are using your words as no more than markers. It is not yet time to start acting the lines and so there is nothing you may usefully contribute.

When you do go to watch them work, go also prepared to learn. Now you will hear just how convincing or un-convincing your dialogue is. Further, you will realise that you've had them say the same thing in the same way too many times. And there are lessons to be learned about timing, or pace, or word order for greater effect. Listen carefully to the remarks the actors make to the director and to each other about the difficulties they encounter in bringing the text alive. And trust their judgement in the matter. They are the ones who have to go out there under the lights with no means of escape and *do* it – while you are comfortably hidden in the dark.

As rehearsals progress, the director will gradually arrange things so that the point of any scene is absolutely clear. And, if you have a good director, you will be astonished at the inventive creation of 'business'. That is the pattern of actions which are performed while the lines are being delivered. You may have wondered in earlier examples why there are so few stage directions. What, you may have wondered, are the actors *doing* all this while. They are doing what the director devises for them to do.

Some directors have marvellous skill in movement, positioning and 'business'. But whether they are good or bad, what must never be questioned is the fact that they are in charge. It is a very difficult job, requiring a high degree of theatrical talent and almost equal degrees of sensitivity and dominance. The sensitivity must be displayed in understanding of the script and dealing with the insecurity of actors. The dominance is essential because nearly a score of artistic temperaments may be involved in the enterprise and one person's decisions must prevail.

With some directors, the sensitivity does not extend to the writer. They are those who are or who wanted to be writers themselves. In spite of that, they are unable to judge a play from the written text. Only when the play is in rehearsal do they discover the thing doesn't work. If you are a new writer, you try to make it work the way they would have written it – if they could write.

More dangerous than these are the 'trampoline' directors. They don't want the play to have a text *as such*. If it can be managed, the performance will be an exhibition of their own talent and very noticeable ability. In order to display the directorial leaps and spins, your play becomes their trampoline.

Most dangerous of all are the 'cause' directors. The reason they decided to do your play at all was that it seemed to them it was advocating a political or social cause in which they are passionate believers. Almost any play can be twisted to support some 'cause'. Thus it becomes a vehicle for the greater good, to your considerable loss.

Perhaps I'm lucky, but though I've heard vivid first hand accounts of directors such as these I've had to work with very few of them. I hope you are as lucky as I have been. But no matter what sort of director you get, your contribution at rehearsals is fairly well defined. When the actors are going through a scene, you sit where you can see and you make notes of anything which strikes you as wrong or odd.

At the end of the scene, and out of earshot of the actors, you discuss these notes with the director. Of course, the director, too, has been making notes and some of them apply to you. For example, both of you may have noted that a particular line is causing difficulty for the actor. It is possible that the line has not been understood. You clarify what you intended. The director may agree with the interpretation and pass it on. But the actor is still in difficulty. There is no virtue in being right if the person who has to do it can't do it. It's better to change the line.

The playwright is always consulted on any proposed change in the text. Some changes are desirable not because of any failing in the actors but because the particular staging of the piece makes lines redundant or confusing. Very often there is good reason to add new lines. It is helpful, therefore, if the playwright does not take up a position at rehearsals which too militantly guards the text. Rather, he should think of himself as the first audience of the performance. That is the function in which he can best serve the actors.

Considering the wealth of creative work done by others in the rehearsal of a play, it seems unfair that the changes or additions become the property of the playwright. You can add them to the script which is going to be sent out for new productions of the same piece. All that's asked in return is a printed acknowledgement in your next programme stating at which theatre the play was first produced.

For the opening night of the first production you will be provided with free tickets for yourself and a decent number of your friends or family. However, I know very few playwrights who actually sit with their friends or family. It is more instructive to sit alone where you've got a good view of the audience as well as the stage. The director will probably be doing the same thing and you could keep each other company.

During a performance listen for the coughs. There are bound to be some but in general people don't cough if their attention is fully held by what is happening on the stage. If there is a prolonged outbreak of coughing, make a mental note of where in the text it started. With a comedy, of course, you also listen for laughs. Note which lines produce laughter and compare that with the next time you watch a performance of the same play. The laughs will come in different places.

But the coughs will come in the same places. The obvious, and valid, deduction is that different things make different audiences laugh – but all audiences are bored by the same things.

With a little practice you can refine your observations. Laughing and coughing are not the only things which audiences do. Indeed they make an odd assortment of much subtler noises, from gurgles to grunts to sighs and even murmurs. What is more, they seem to do it in unison. Gradually you will be able to interpret what those noises mean and you'll have their cause in mind when writing your next play.

A further variation which may be observed is the reaction which is conditioned by the size of the audience – I mean their numbers. Suppose it's a comedy and there are two nights when the house is half full. They won't laugh very much on either night. But if it were possible to get the same people together on *one* night you'd have a packed house and they would laugh a great deal.

Alternatively, if you put the original number in a smaller theatre they too would laugh much more. So it is not just a matter of numbers. It depends more on there being few spaces around them. Thus, it is far better to stage a comedy in a small theatre than in a large one.

Reaction to drama is more difficult to judge in the auditorium but you can certainly get a clear impression when they come out at the interval. If they've enjoyed it they talk a lot, not necessarily about the play. And they come out slowly. If they have not enjoyed it they come quickly and silently. And they seem reluctant to go back.

104

Next morning, or very shortly thereafter, you will be able to check if your observations were sound. You'll be able to read what the critics think of your play.

It is a fact of life that if you are a new playwright, any failure will be blamed on you and any success will be attributed to the actors or director. That balance will be redressed later when you are established and the cast or director are new. Then when you write a bad play *they* will get the blame. Either way it is important to keep in mind that in most instances it is quite impossible for critics to separate a new play from the production of it. In performance, every aspect is intertwined with another. It is a unified, coherent structure. That is what all the preparation and rehearsal were aimed at achieving. So there is no point in feeling downcast or elated at critical reaction. By then, the play has not been yours for some time – and it will never be entirely yours again.

Chapter Ten

The business of being a playwright needs careful planning. In my opinion your first piece of major planning is to provide yourself with a word-processor and learn to use it. You see, apart from the ability to run off cheap face copies of the script (few theatres return scripts) there is the ability to convert the script for other markets with the minimum of effort. I'll demonstrate how that is done in what follows.

Most new writers start with the much simpler goal of just getting a play produced. They offer the new script to a West End management and after what seems an interminable time the offer is declined. One reason is that the West End takes even fewer chances now than it ever did. Almost every play which is staged on Shaftesbury Avenue was originally staged by somebody else – usually by a repertory or a fringe theatre.

Now, fringe theatres exist in a number of cities – but perhaps you don't live in a city. So – couldn't you just send the script to a fringe theatre in a city? You could, but bear in mind that there are more writers in cities than elsewhere. Scores of them milling around *in person* with their own scripts *in hand.* And they'll have the edge because they are on the spot and the directors can see and talk to them.

Theatre runs on personal contact. And theatre directors do plays by people they know – or know *of.* If you already have a personal contact, milk it for all it's worth.

If you just don't know anybody in the theatre, what I recommend is the two-play ploy. This applies in approaching civic/repertory theatres and depends on the fact that they are supported by public money. It is part of their duty to nurture and reflect the community which they serve. That means making your first play a local play. In whatever town or district you live, something remarkable has happened in the past, or someone famous has lived there before you. Write 'play one' about it, or him, or her.

There is always an opening, every year or two, for some new treatment for even an oft-told tale. This time *you* tell it. If you tell it well, or even passably, you are in. 'Play one' goes on and during rehearsals you get to know the people who are running the theatre. When that is accomplished, you spring 'play two' on them. And you do that while your first play is on and you have unlimited access to the theatre.

Naturally, you complete 'play two' before you offer 'play one' – but you don't tell anybody that. If you do, you won't be commissioned to write the play you've already written. It is never too early to start being commissioned. That means interesting a director in the idea. There shouldn't be much difficulty, for 'play two' is the play you really wanted to write. It is the play I've been trying to help you to write. And, if you are wise, it is a play aimed at a much wider public than 'play one' and capable of easy adaptation to radio, television and fiction.

There is longer term benefit in the initial deception over the fact that the play is already written. You will feel certain of being able to deliver on time. The fact that you undoubtedly can will do wonders for your reputation. It will make it easier to obtain further commissions.

Initially, though, your income is from 'play one'. And it is likely to come from the Arts Council. They, too, are dispensers of public money with a duty to nurture all the things 'play one' so plainly celebrates. The Arts Council play commissioning scheme at the moment offers a minimum fee and guaranteed royalties totalling £2,500. A three week run is likely to earn you a further £1,500 above the advance royalties. The application for commissioning fees must be made by a theatre director on your behalf.

So, 'play one' has been successfully produced (local plays are *always* successful – in the locality) and 'play two' is scheduled for production. Now is the time to approach an agency with a view to their handling the contract for 'play two'. Send the agent a copy of the play and outline what you've done and what is in prospect.

If they don't take you on immediately, handle the contract

yourself. 'Play two' is likely to be governed by the TMA Minimum Terms Contract which was agreed last year by the Theatre Managers Association. The fact that it is not your first play enables you to ensure that you are paid more than the minimum. And here is the strength of going for a commission – you can get the theatre to spend money which they will make some effort to recoup. They can do that only if they stage the play.

I am not allowed to tell you the specific sums involved but you will be provided with – or should certainly ask for – a contract blank on which the various minima are printed. Among the financial stipulations of this and any other stage contract are these:

The 'Consideration' – which is the sum payable on signature of contract; the bulk of which is *not* set against royalties and is non-returnable in any event.

The Box Office Royalty – which is the percentage of the ticket sales due to you and the guaranteed royalty regardless of attendance figures. When the earnings reach a certain level, a higher percentage is paid.

The Acceptance Fee – which is paid on acceptance of the play for production and will be set against royalties.

The Attendance Fee – which is a daily rate paid for the author's attendance at rehearsals, within reason.

Expenses – in connection with attendance at production meetings and rehearsals.

If you are now represented by an agency, they will deal with the contract and collect the money for you. Indeed, all money (apart from Attendance and Expenses) will be sent to the agency who will deduct 10% before passing it on to you. They will also be doing their best to line up another production of the same play.

While all that is going on, you still have all the other saleable rights to consider. For the stage contract leaves you in possession of all other rights and there is no point in waiting until the first stage licence expires before making use of them.

In the following pages there are examples of how the same script is adapted to suit the various possibilities. I've used another scene from *The Only Street* because the characters and situation are already familiar to the reader and the purpose here is largely to set out format and notes. The value of a word-processor becomes apparent in that I typed the dialogue only once but was able to reproduce it in four different versions. If you have your play on disc, you can do the same.

We start with the original scene in stage script.

As anticipated, when RICHARD tells KATE about his brother's strange malady she comes to see him. They have a rather painful scene together in which MARTIN makes it clear that their affair is over. They are then interrupted by MARTIN's mother, BEATRICE.

STAGE – 'The Only Street'

MARTIN	Mother, may I introduce Kate – a quite undomesticated girl of good education – with whom I have been living, and dying, by inches.
KATE	I had the impression you enjoyed it.
MARTIN	Enjoying it doesn't alter the fact. (TO BEATRICE) But that we have enjoyed it is something you should know – and now can see why.
BEATRICE	I have seen . . . Kate, before now.
MARTIN	Had her pointed out, you mean.
KATE	(TO BEATRICE) Did you?
MARTIN	Of course she did. Thought of reporting you. To the NSPCC.

He gives a bellow of laughter.

Because there's not a pick *on* me. Well, that's my little chore done.

He moves to door.

Too bad spiderman Richard is otherwise engaged, but what with this gathering, the prospect of bath and a renegade doctor imminent, my mornings are getting crowded enough.

EXIT MARTIN

BEATRICE   He's feverish, I think.

> BEATRICE and KATE look at each other. KATE turns away and BEATRICE, watching her, sits.

KATE   Maybe.
A "rescue operation". To rescue him I suppose. That's what he said.

BEATRICE   I've never much listened to what he said. He talks a lot of nonsense, y'know, at times.

KATE   But a rescue would make sense.

BEATRICE   If he was drownin', maybe.

> KATE, to the surprise of BEATRICE, makes a small start towards the door but suppresses it at once.

KATE   Will he be all right in there?

BEATRICE   Havin' a bath!

KATE   It might affect his . . . temperature . . . Affect his balance. And if the door's locked . . .

BEATRICE   There's no lock on the door.

> BEATRICE gives KATE an assessing stare as she digs out her cigarettes and prepares to light up. She nods.

You're a teacher.

KATE   Yes. Very young children.

BEATRICE   He was lucky there.

110

KATE	Pardon?
BEATRICE	A good steady wage, I mean. He can't make much with what he plays at.
KATE	Oh, he makes quite a lot.
BEATRICE	I'm talkin' about money, not brooches.
KATE	I thought . . . no. No, he doesn't sell much. But he could sell more. He makes very beautiful jewellery.
BEATRICE	Maybe if he didn't satisfy himself so much he'd sell more. He's finicky. Always was. What he does he does to please himself instead of tryin' to please whoever might buy it.
KATE	Yes, that's true.
BEATRICE	There's no need to tell *me* what's true about Martin.
KATE	You're right. Is that better?
BEATRICE	Hmm.
KATE	Mrs Doyle . . .

> BEATRICE looks at her earnestly
> – as though that was a reply.

Mrs Doyle, I was going to . . .

BEATRICE	Yes. I heard ya. And I think we could . . . and better together than separately.

Adapting for Radio

I'd recommend that the first adaptation you attempt should
be for radio. The BBC publishes a booklet called *Writing
For The BBC*. It is regularly updated and provides
information on current requirements, play lengths for sound
broadcasting, addresses of editorial departments and examples
of various script formats.

If you compare the following version of the scene with the stage version you will note that there is very little change in the actual dialogue. But, right away, there is an indication of what you must bear in mind. Movement in the room will be suggested by the distances the actors are from the microphone. The direction (CLOSE) places MARTIN in relation to BEATRICE, who is standing near him, and their distance from KATE, who is over at the window. At (APPROACHES) KATE's voice gets louder during the speech and we know she is moving over to MARTIN and his mother.

It will be appreciated that you do not try to duplicate the actions and movements which were performed on the stage. On radio the actors do not need to move nearly as much, so you introduce movement either for variety or to make a dramatic point. Everything is aimed at enabling the listener to 'visualise' what is happening.

I've added 'Mrs Doyle' to KATE's second speech. On the stage we can see who she's talking to, on radio it is wise to place identifying markers of this sort. But not every time. If there are only two people in the scene the listener knows that it's one or the other talking and can recognise the voice.

The 'stage directions' now become 'sound directions' and are always set out thus. The door will not be opened by the actor but by someone doing 'effects'. Similarly, when BEATRICE sighs as she lowers herself into a chair, the actress will not sit down at all and the chair creak will be provided by somebody else. The direction enables the actress to know how to say the speech to give a 'sitting down' sound and instructs the effects man on what sound is required.

Sometimes it is wise to insert extra lines for clarity – as near the top of page 115. On the stage BEATRICE interrupted KATE's speech with a look. Here she does it with 'Huh?' This covers what would be, to the listener, an inexplicable pause.

RADIO – 'The Only Street'

MARTIN   (CLOSE) Mother, may I introduce Kate –
            a quite undomesticated girl of good
            education – with whom I have been living,
            and dying, by inches.

KATE	(DISTANT) I had the impression you enjoyed it.
MARTIN	Enjoying it doesn't alter the fact. But that we have enjoyed it is something you should know – and now can see why.
BEATRICE	(CLOSE) I have seen . . . Kate, before now.
MARTIN	Had her pointed out, you mean.
KATE	(APPROACHING) Did you, Mrs Doyle?
MARTIN	Of course she did. Thought of reporting you. To the NSPCC – because there's not a pick *on* me. Well, that's my little chore done. (RECEDING) Too bad spiderman Richard is otherwise engaged, but what with this gathering . . .

(SOUND OF DOOR OPENING)

. . . the prospect of bath and a renegade doctor imminent, my mornings are getting crowded enough.

(SOUND OF DOOR CLOSING)

BEATRICE	He's feverish, I think.

(CHAIR BANGED INTO NEW POSITION)

KATE	Maybe. A 'rescue operation'. To rescue him I suppose. That's what he said.

(BEATRICE LOWERS HER-SELF INTO CHAIR WHICH CREAKS)

BEATRICE	(SIGHING) I've never much listened to what he said. He talks a lot of nonsense, y'know, at times.
KATE	But a rescue would make sense.
BEATRICE	If he was drownin', maybe.

113

KATE	Will he be all right in there?
BEATRICE	Havin' a bath!
KATE	It might affect his . . . temperature . . . (RECEDING QUICKLY) Affect his balance. And if the door's locked . . .
BEATRICE	(LOUDLY) There's no lock on the door.
KATE	(APPROACHING) Oh! He should be all right then.
BEATRICE	You're a teacher.
KATE	Yes. Very young children.
BEATRICE	He was lucky there.
KATE	Pardon?
BEATRICE	A good steady wage, I mean. He can't make much with what he plays at.
KATE	Oh, he makes quite a lot.
BEATRICE	I'm talkin' about money, not brooches.
KATE	I thought . . . no. No, he doesn't sell much. But he could sell more. He makes very beautiful jewellery.

(RUSTLE AS BEATRICE SEARCHES IN HER APRON POCKET FOR CIGARETTES AND MATCHES)

BEATRICE	Maybe if he didn't satisfy himself so much he'd sell more. He's finicky. Always was. What he does he does to please himself instead of tryin' to please whoever might buy it.

(BEATRICE OPENS CIGARETTE PACKET)

KATE	Yes, that's true.
BEATRICE	There's no need to tell *me* what's true about Martin.

114

KATE	You're right. Is that better?

(<u>MATCH STRUCK</u>)

KATE	Mrs Doyle . . .
BEATRICE	Huh?
KATE	Mrs Doyle, I was going to . . .
BEATRICE	Yes. I heard ya. And I think we could . . . and better together than separately.

Adapting for Television

Whereas the following example is useful in developing an existing text, I would strongly recommend another, very helpful, book in this series before you attempt a television adaptation. *The Way To Write For Television* by Eric Paice deals expertly with all the hazards and requirements and is written with great clarity and liveliness.

The first thing which ought to be explained is the scene number and heading. The reason we're at Scene 23 while still in the first act of the stage play is that we did not start with the opening scene of the stage play. In adapting to television I started with events which are only reported on the stage. That was a whole exterior sequence which showed what happened at the end of the scene reproduced here.

When MARTIN escapes from the house he runs to the building site where RICHARD is working and, still barefoot, starts climbing up the high-rise skeletal structure to reach his brother. He gets stuck and RICHARD has to rescue him by abseiling down with the safety harness by which MARTIN can be lowered to the ground.

The heading, INT / BEDROOM / DAY indicates that this is an interior scene, that the interior is the bedroom – which is likely to be a set and not a film location, and that the events occur in daylight. This scene is followed by an interior, STAIRWAY & LANDING which is likely to be a real location and not a set. Since these two scenes cannot be shot one after the other, the reason for the notation becomes plain. All the scene numbers pertaining to one place can be filmed together.

115

It will be noted that, as mentioned earlier, television scenes are much shorter than stage scenes. And the action is fragmented. Here we see what MARTIN does when he goes out of the bedroom and that is relevantly intercut with the scene between BEATRICE and KATE continuing.

The reference to the lock on the bathroom door is cut, not only because the audience can see the bathroom but because MARTIN clearly has no intention of having a bath.

The 'directions' in this instance are self-contained notes on what the camera looks at, and in which order. Scene 26, for example, has three camera positions: we see MARTIN looking into the bath, then we look into the bath, then – from the other side of the bathroom – we see MARTIN turn to the door.

TELEVISION – 'The Moth and the Spiderman'

Sc. 23   INT / BEDROOM / DAY
- -

BEATRICE confronts MARTIN and KATE.

> MARTIN: Mother, may I introduce Kate
> – a quite undomesticated girl of good
> education – with whom I have been living,
> and dying, by inches.

> KATE: I had the impression you enjoyed
> it.

> MARTIN: Enjoying it doesn't alter the
> fact.
> (TO BEATRICE) But we have – and now
> you can see why.

BEATRICE gives KATE an assessing stare.

KATE shows some impatience.

> BEATRICE: I have seen . . . Kate, before
> now.

> MARTIN: Had her pointed out, you mean.

> KATE: (TO BEATRICE) Did you?

116

MARTIN: Of course she did. Thought of reporting you. To the NSPCC.

MARTIN gives a bellow of laughter.

MARTIN: Because there's not a pick *on* me. Well, that's my little chore done.

MARTIN moves to door.

MARTIN: Too bad spiderman Richard is otherwise engaged, but what with this gathering, the prospect of bath and a renegade doctor imminent, my mornings are getting crowded enough.

MARTIN goes out.

Sc. 24   INT / STAIRWAY & LANDING / DAY
- -

MARTIN crosses landing and opens bathroom door.

Sc. 25   INT / BEDROOM / DAY
- -

Resume Sc. 23

BEATRICE: He's feverish, I think.

BEATRICE and KATE look at each other.

KATE turns away.

BEATRICE moves tray from chair on to bed and sits in chair.

KATE: Maybe. A 'rescue operation'. To rescue him I suppose. That's what he said.

BEATRICE takes out her cigarettes and lights up.

BEATRICE: I've never much listened to what he said. He talks a lot of nonsense, y'know, at times.

117

KATE: But a rescue would make sense.

BEATRICE: If he was drownin', maybe.

Sc. 26   INT / BATHROOM / DAY

MARTIN, still dressed, smiling, watches water pour into bath.

We look closer and see that the plug is not in position.

MARTIN, after a moment watching water pour away, turns to open bathroom door.

Sc. 27   INT / BEDROOM / DAY

Resume Sc. 25

BEATRICE: You're a teacher.

KATE, looking out of window, turns to face BEATRICE.

KATE: Yes. Very young children.

Sc. 28   INT / STAIRWAY & LANDING / DAY

MARTIN, very cautiously, descends the stair.

Sc. 29   INT / BEDROOM / DAY

Resume Sc. 27

BEATRICE: He was lucky there.

KATE: Pardon?

BEATRICE: A good steady wage, I mean. He can't make much with what he plays at.

KATE: Oh, he makes quite a lot.

BEATRICE flicks cigarette ash into cup.

BEATRICE: I'm talkin' about money, not brooches.

KATE: I thought . . . no. No, he doesn't sell much. But he could sell more. He makes very beautiful jewellery.

BEATRICE: Maybe if he didn't satisfy himself so much he'd sell more. He's finicky. Always was. What he does he does to please himself, instead of tryin' to please whoever might buy it.

KATE: Yes, that's true.

BEATRICE: There's no need to tell *me* what's true about Martin.

KATE: You're right. Is that better?

Sc. 30   EXT / SLUM STREET / DAY
- -

MARTIN runs wildly along the broken pavement.

Passers-by turn to stare at the barefoot young man dressed only in flapping shirt and trousers.

Sc. 31   INT / BEDROOM / DAY
- -

Resume Sc. 29

KATE: Mrs Doyle . . .

BEATRICE looks at her earnestly – as though that was a reply.

KATE: Mrs Doyle, I was going to . . .

BEATRICE: I think we could. And better together than separately.

119

Adapting for Fiction

In my opinion, this is the easiest adaptation to accomplish, as far as the dialogue is concerned. But a story or a novel is not all dialogue. You must also set down how things look, what the characters think and how they behave. However, if you have been through stage rehearsals, and been on location for the television version, and argued through long discussions for them and the radio version, there will be very little you do not know about every moment of the action.

Even so, you will note that I haven't described the scene of MARTIN in the bathroom. It would break the continuity and 'build' of the scene between the women. It was put in just for television because in that medium there is no virtue in building scenes but there is great emphasis on keeping the camera busy.

Here, too, I have cut or shortened some of the lines. They are those which most depended on how the actor could deliver them. The reader is not an actor.

And though it is not apparent in this scene there were many occasions elsewhere in the adaptation where it was necessary to rid the dialogue of any subtlety whatsoever. Time and again my publisher's editor made it clear that fiction cannot afford delicate nuances in dialogue. The sort of thing which an actor can do with good lines is just wasted on the reader. That, I think, is what I regret most about writing fiction after so many years of writing for the stage. You see the habit is bred in me that it is wrong to overwrite. Instinctively aware that I must leave space for the actor to stand and deliver, I am loath to add what the reader of fiction has come to expect. And the reader clearly expects the piece to be overwritten.

It is because I'm just a new boy at fiction that I cannot offer more specific advice in this instance. I've tried to show you how you can turn your idea into a play but I really cannot offer any practical help on how you may turn your play into a book. All I can do is demonstrate how the same dialogue is integrated and arranged for publication. But the publication itself may be of further help to you as a playwright. *The Jewel Maker*, published by Hamish Hamilton,

120

is a collection of five long stories, all narrated by a playwright and each dealing with some aspect of stage work.

FICTION – The Jewel Maker

'Mother, may I introduce Kate – a quite undomesticated girl of good education – with whom I have been living, and dying, by inches.'

'I had the impression you enjoyed it,' the girl said.

'Enjoying it doesn't alter the fact.' To his mother he added soberly, 'But that we have enjoyed it is something you should know – and now can see why.'

'I have seen . . . Kate, before now,' his mother allowed.

'Had her pointed out, you mean.'

'Did you?' Kate asked incredulously.

'Of course she did. Thought of reporting you to the NSPCC – because there's not a pick *on* me.' He gave a bellow of laughter and swaggered to the door. 'Well, that's my little chore done. Too bad spiderman Richard is otherwise engaged, but what with this gathering, the prospect of bath and a renegade doctor imminent, my mornings are getting crowded enough.' He went out and closed the door behind him.

Beatrice shook her head wearily. 'He's feverish, I think.'

'Maybe. A "rescue operation". To rescue him I suppose. That's what he said.'

'I've never much listened to what he said. He talks a lot of nonsense, y'know, at times.'

'But a rescue would make sense.'

'If he was drownin', maybe.'

'Will he be all right in there?'

'Havin' a bath!'

'It might affect his . . . temperature . . . Affect his balance. And if the door's locked . . .'

'There's no lock on the door.' Having cleared away everything that would create an actual obstruction, Beatrice decided the room was tidy enough. She folded her arms and nodded to Kate. 'You're a teacher.'

'Yes. Very young children.'

'He was lucky there.'

'Pardon?'

'A good steady wage, I mean. He can't make much with what he plays at.'

'Oh, he makes quite a lot.'

'I'm talkin' about money, not brooches.'

'I thought . . . no. No, he doesn't sell much. But he could sell more. He makes very beautiful jewellery,' Kate said.

'Maybe if he didn't satisfy himself so much he'd sell more. He's finicky. Always was. What he does he does to please himself instead of tryin' to please whoever might buy it.'

'Yes, that's true.'

'There's no need to tell *me* what's true about Martin.'

'You're right.' The girl hastily corrected any impression that she had a mind of her own. 'Is that better?'

'Hmm.' Beatrice moved the tray on to the bed and sat in the vacated chair. There established, she dug out her cigarettes and lit up.

'Mrs Doyle,' Kate began. Beatrice gave her a quick glance through shrewd eyes crinkled against tobacco smoke. But she said nothing and Kate tried again, 'Mrs Doyle, I was going to . . .'

'Yes. I heard ya. And I think we could . . . and better together than separately.'

Finally, I would like to offer you the best and most important piece of advice. It is that you should read as many plays as you can lay hands on and see as many plays as you can afford. Better: read the play you are going to see, even if you have to read it in a published book.

Of course, it is much more useful if you can get hold of the script which your nearest theatre intends to produce. Read it with great care, then go and see the production. The most effective key to writing for the stage is a love of the stage.